DOMO ARIGATO, MISTER ROBOTO

COMPANION CHRONICLES VOLUME 6

JOSHUA TODD JAMES

PRAISE FOR JOSHUA TODD JAMES

"SOME ANIMALS is a nonstop sci-fi thrill ride that will keep you reading well into the night. Joshua Todd James fills the page with cinematic action scenes and snappy dialogue, all anchored by a compelling protagonist who reflects so much of who we are today."

MIKE NGUYEN LE
(SCREENWRITER/PRODUCER)
PATIENT Z, DARK SUMMER, W.M.D

"Doing noir as sci-fi is a real challenge, and this ambitious book pulls it off!"

DAVID GERROLD, HUGO & NEBULA AWARD-WINNING AUTHOR OF THE MARTIAN CHILD, HELLA, & THE MAN WHO FOLDED HIMSELF

"Joshua Todd James has created a compelling protagonist, a fascinating story universe, and a suspenseful mystery, all-in-one, in his new novel SOME ANIMALS. Think of it as sci-fi nitro in book form. Highly recommended!"

SCOTT MYERS, SCREENWRITER (K-9) AUTHOR OF THE PROTAGONIST'S JOURNEY, PROFESSOR AT DEPAUL UNIVERSITY AND HOST OF GOINTOTHESTORY.COM

"SOME ANIMALS blew my mind. Joshua is the master of moralistic pathos. It's a pathos steeped in a personal code of ethics in each of his characters. Joshua's brilliance is in setting these characters careening down a track fueled by their pathos, and the fun happens when characters with opposing drives collide in an action-packed train wreck of ethics, desires, and dreams. Do. Not. Miss. This. Book."

ATO ESSANDOH, ACTOR (STAR OF NETFLIX'S ALTERED CARBON, AWAY, AMAZON'S TALES FROM THE LOOP, HBO'S VINYL, AND MANY MORE.)

"Joshua Todd James delivers a one-of-a-kind Sci-Fi thrill ride. The depth of its characters and its world are remarkable, especially given how quickly it reads."

NATHAN GRAHAM DAVIS, AUTHOR OF MALICE AND MISTLETOE

"I started reading SOME ANIMALS at 7 AM and didn't stop until I was finished. Joshua Todd James has created a vibrant, fiery futuristic world that we instantly believe in, and characters that hook us deep for this truly wild ride. But this is much more than a cracking good 'Who done it?' It's a story that breaks both boundaries and stereotypes all along the way. Start reading. You won't put it down."

NAOMI WALLACE, PLAYWRIGHT, SCREENWRITER AND MACARTHUR FELLOW (AKA THE GENIUS GRANT)

"From the opening lines of 'Some Animals, ' Joshua Todd James creates a compelling narrative and gripping mystery that you won't want to put down."

TESS RAFFERTY, AUTHOR OF RECIPE FOR DISASTER & UNDER THE TUSCAN GUN

"I love sci-fi, and I love hardboiled detective stories. This is both, but it's even more. Sci-fi has always been the best place to take on real-world issues, and Joshua Todd James takes on a lot of those in SOME ANIMALS. In this book, he serves up a strong cocktail, shaken from Chandler and Asimov, leaving me with the impression that someone just punched me in the face with a new cut of BLADE RUNNER."

YURI LOWENTHAL, ACTOR
MARVEL'S SPIDER-MAN, NARUTO, BEN 10, RAVE MASTER, LEGION OF SUPERHEROES

"Joshua Todd James is a beautiful writer whose compelling, intelligent, and evocative sci-fi brings to mind the work of Isaac Asimov and Andy Weir. SOME ANIMALS weaves a propulsive plot that keeps you turning the pages with the themes that make for our finest speculative fiction—among them, what it means to be human. This exciting story is not one to be missed!"

MARTIN AGUILERA, AUTHOR AND SCREENWRITER, NETFLIX'S THE CRAVING

"SOME ANIMALS is a sci-fi novella that had me smiling throughout. It's fun. It's smart. It's thought-provoking, and most of all it's entertaining as all get out!"

BILL RODEMEYER, CO-AUTHOR OF THE NOVELS JUVENILE X, SUCKERFISH CITY AND TWILIGHT PULP–SHORT READS FOR TWISTED MINDS

"SOME ANIMALS is an intriguing exploration of a future that is moving, tense and which reflects, heart-breakingly so, upon our present-day society."

DWAYNE ALEXANDER SMITH, BESTSELLING AUTHOR OF FORTY ACRES AND THE UNKIND HOURS

"The Fugitive meets Blade Runner, SOME ANIMALS is a fast-paced, near-future Science Fiction thriller about an android "companion" accused of his human's murder and goes on the run, relentlessly pursued by an obsessed detective, and it really delivers. As he searches for the real killer, he learns what it means to be human... and inhumane."

WILLIAM C. MARTELL, SCREENWRITER (19 PRODUCED FILMS THUS AND STILL COUNTING) AND AUTHOR OF THE HUGELY POPULAR BLUE BOOK SERIES ON SCREENWRITING

"The best stories are always a sort of mix of genres. And that's exactly what Joshua Todd James has done with SOME ANIMALS. He's created a tasty genre burrito that reminded me of some of the best old-school sci-fi and detective stories, then spiced it up with several issues relevant to today."

CHAD LAW,
SCREENWRITER/PRODUCER,
DRIVE HARD, DAYLIGHT'S END,
THE SHADOW EFFECT,
BLACKWATER, DAY OF HEROES

"Finally, it happened. I've long wanted to begin and end a book in one setting. SOME ANIMALS is that book. What is a Companion? What is a human being? Joshua Todd James reminds me of Heinlein, merging intelligence and story with effortless precision while subtly confronting tough questions in a hugely entertaining tale. This is a terrific, unexpected work."

JOEL EISENBERG, AUTHOR OF
THE CHRONICLES OF ARA

"I wish Joshua Todd James had been around when I was reading young adult novels because SOME ANIMALS is superb, and Jacob Kind is a memorable protagonist. He's a Companion, an android designed to serve the needs of his owners. On the run from corrupt police, falsely accused of the murder of his owner, Jacob discovers that he's more than an android -- that process of learning who you really are will resonate with readers. This is compulsively readable and strongly recommended."

DANIEL KEYS MORAN, AUTHOR OF EMERALD EYES, THE LONG RUN, THE LAST DANCER & THE A.I. WAR, BOOK ONE: THE BIG BOOST

"Some Animals is an exciting and propulsive sci-fi thriller. Don't miss it!"

KI YU WU, WRITER/PRODUCER (THE FLASH, CARNIVAL ROW, HANNIBAL)

INTRODUCTION

Synthetic Companion Jacob Kind's last memory was of crashing a truck on a dark night road with a bullet in his shoulder. Rescued by a retired doctor and his wife and brought to their farm, he struggles with an addiction to opiates that has crippled him. As he undergoes a hellish detox, Jacob knows his very presence puts his rescuers, pro-synthetic advocates, in real danger. A very bad man, Munson Tolliver, is coming for him.

But Larkin Finn, the man Jacob's adopted mother sent him to find, is also somewhere in the area, and he must find the man before Tolliver finds them both.

Will Jacob, in his diminished capacity, be able to protect his new-found friends? Will he live up to his promise to serve and protect humanity?

Cover design by Todd Alcott

Artwork by Rizal Abdillah

Sylvia's Last Breath art by Doan Trang.

For any and everyone who's ever had to make a final stand.

PROLOGUE

I WAS NOT BORN as you were.

I was not dragged from a womb, kicking and screaming, held and fed until I calmed. I did not arrive in this world as a baby. I am made of living tissue, as you are; I breathe, hunger, thirst, and do everything you do. I bleed like you, though my blood is green rather than red as yours. I am a synthetic person, manufactured in a factory, but yet a living being with the same desires, needs, and weaknesses that you have.

I simply did not begin life in the same fashion as my human equivalents.

I was birthed exactly as you see me now, as a fully realized male. I was created in a lab by a man and sold from a store by another man, but I was purchased by a woman who cared for me and taught me about the world, life, and even my sense of self.

Her name was Sylvia Kind, and I'm forever in her debt.

Sylvia was, I later found out, expressly against the selling of synthetic beings, though she never communicated why she acquired me in spite of her feelings on the matter. She simply loved and supported me and encouraged and challenged me to think for myself.

Sylvia was in pursuit of someone, a man she recently discovered was named Larkin Finn. On the very same night she acquired that information, Sylvia was attacked and stabbed in her condo by a masked man. I fought off her attacker, but Sylvia passed away in my arms.

I sketched a picture of her attacker, who I could tell from touch had no hair anywhere on his body. The police identified him as one Munson Tolliver. The problem was that Munson Tolliver had been shot and killed by the very police detective questioning me six months previously. So they didn't believe my story.

Though my kind was designed to be incapable of committing violence against humans, the authorities believed I murdered Sylvia. Corrupt police officers attempted to take my life in the station house, and they shot one of their own as a result. Police officers died, and they blamed me for that as well. And while that happened, I discovered that, in spite of how I was built, I did somehow have the capacity to injure humans.

I escaped and went on the run; with the help of some local gang members, I had my manufacturer's tag removed, and now I'm free.

Free, except that I have the manufacturer's agents after me and the police, in particular a very tough homicide detective named Abigail Moore, who believes I murdered her partner, also in pursuit.

I'm on my own, on the run, and determined to find who murdered my primary and why, who this Larkin Finn is, and, above all else, my promise to Sylvia... which is to protect and serve humanity at all costs.

My name is Jacob Kind, and I am a Companion.

ONE

I HEARD birds singing when I woke, which was the first sign that I was not dead. If I were dead, I doubt birds would be singing or I could hear them. This led me to realize that I couldn't recall the last time I'd even heard a bird sing, though I'd spent much of the late summer and fall outdoors in upstate New York, and birds were plentiful in the area. I'm sure they had been singing during that terrible period of my existence. I just hadn't been able to hear them because I was fighting to the death in a box while being cheered on by humans drunk on whiskey, cruelty, and arrogance.

I took a breath, let it out, and orientated myself. I was in a bed, a very nice, soft bed. There was a closed window with the curtains drawn open, and bright, warm sunlight streamed. It snowed outside, and big fat flakes drifted down, slow and careful, as though navigating their way into life for the first time. A starling sat on the window sill, not but four feet away from me, and sang for the snowfall. Its song had woken me.

I tried to move, and pain shot through my shoulder. I glanced over and saw it was bandaged. I remembered a man had shot me after I had burned down a factory that used synthetics, like myself, as slave labor. I'd gotten caught in the middle of a dispute between the company and an environmental advocacy group when everything went to shit; a woman I thought I could love was murdered; I murdered the person responsible and later confronted Munson Tolliver once again, only to be separated by a river of fire.

Wounded, I'd driven away from that mess and kept going until I lost enough blood to lose consciousness. And woke up in this bed, a bird singing to me on the window sill, my shoulder bandaged, and an IV in my arm, attached to a bag of saline solution on a stand. Green blood seeped through the bandages. That meant that whoever had patched me up knew I wasn't human, knew I was a runaway synthetic Companion, and yet did not call the police nor the Companion corporation on me.

I took stock of where I was. It was a bedroom, but it had an older feel. Wood paneling on the walls, antique chairs next to an equally old chest of drawers, and just the overall whiff of classic work around the room. From the sound of things outside, I didn't get the sense that this was a city or a town; it felt like a farmhouse. I tried to sit up again, but the pain in my shoulder was immense. I gasped and fell back. Beyond the piercing agony of my injury, I felt something far worse. A thirst, but not for water or any fluid. I desperately needed my pills.

My gear sat on a nearby chair. The bottle of pills would be in my jacket. I tried sitting up, but everything blurred before I could get elevated, and I passed out again.

THE NEXT TIME I WOKE, I heard rock and roll music and someone moving around. I opened my eyes and saw a pretty woman with red hair done up in two braids, stacking dirty laundry next to my bed. She hummed along to the song playing in another part of the house. I heard some of the lyrics, something about too much time on my hands, but I didn't recognize the music.

It hit me then that what I wore when I woke up had changed. I'd worn blue flannel pajamas before and now wore red ones. The soiled blue ones rested on top of her laundry basket. This woman had changed my clothes, somehow, but I was so helpless I couldn't feel embarrassed, at least not yet. That would surely come later. She'd changed the bedding, too. And I noted a bedpan on the floor, filled with urine that I had no doubt supplied myself. The sight of that made me ashamed of myself.

Her age could have been anywhere from her late twenties to her early thirties. She had freckles, I noted, and green eyes. Slender, in a long skirt and a tied-off man's work shirt over a tank top, thick socks on her feet. The socks, I saw, had the face of a kitten adorning the toes. That meant the cat's whiskers would wiggle when she wriggled her toes. I found that very touching for some reason, and it nearly made me cry. I know not why.

I wondered if I'd been found by one of those fringe religious groups that espoused technology and the like. My mother Sylvia and I had watched a film once on the classic film channel about a detective who got shot and ended up on one of these farms. She loved the film and never tired of viewing it. I couldn't remember the title, but it had a movie star who was one of Sylvia's favorites; he also starred in another classic from the same era, Raiders of the Lost Ark.

I couldn't remember the name of the film, which worried me. I usually remembered everything I'd seen with my eyes. But I could not recall the movie's title, no matter how much effort I put into it. The name of the religious community in the film finally came to my mind: Amish, it had been called Amish. They dressed in plain clothes and did not use electricity or power tools, for some reason that was never clear to me, even back when I first watched the movie. They were real, Sylvia told me, and still existed but in far smaller numbers.

As I contemplated the above, the woman in my room turned and saw I was awake. She smiled happily.

"Well, hello there, Sleepy. Look who's awake! Larry? Larry, our patient is back among the conscious! Larry will be in to check on you in a minute. How are you feeling?"

"Are you Amish?" I said, my voice barely a croak.

"I'm sorry, no. My name is Eve, but everyone calls me Evie. This Amish person, is he or she a friend of yours? Can we call them?"

"No," I managed to get out as I struggled to sit up, then fell back, too exhausted to try again or explain what I meant.

"I'm sorry," I said.

"For what?"

"For... for..." I pointed to the soiled pajamas in her basket.

"This? This is nothing. It's just waste. We all do it, and that's the thing about waste: it wipes off. What's your name?" Evie asked, her hand on her belly.

"Jacob. Who did..." I gestured to the IV and bandages.

"Larry fixed you up, he's a doctor. We found you in a ditch by the road on our way home, and I guess it was your lucky day because Larry said if we'd found you even a few minutes later, you'd be dead. Larry?"

"Coming!"

I sighed. I had so many questions that my brain felt full. What I needed to clear the cobwebs was tucked away in my jacket. Before I could ask Evie for it, Larry entered the room carrying a clear plastic bag filled with red blood. The bandaid on his inner elbow indicated that the fresh blood was his. He held it up, triumphant.

"Another nourishing bag for our boy! Hello there, how are you feeling?"

"He told me his name is Jacob," Evie said. "He asked for someone named Amish."

"No, I..." I began before my mouth dried out.

"Honey, he probably thought you were Amish; it's a religious sect, and the women in that religion wear long skirts like you're wearing now," Larry said. "As far as I know, very few Amish people are left. We are not Amish, my friend. Neither of us is religious. Hi Jacob, my name is Dr. Lawrence Farmer; you can call me Larry; everyone does, and I'm glad you're alive. It was a coin toss for you, there for a couple of days. We were worried we were going to lose you. Evie, can you get him some water, room temp? His throat likely feels like sandpaper at the moment. Let me plug this in; lucky for you, I'm a universal donor, my blood type."

Evie smiled and bustled out as Larry hung the blood bag on the stand.

"You can't... give me that... I'm a..."

"Synthetic, yes, I know. I saw the green blood. This may surprise you, but synthetic blood is compatible with universal donor blood. It won't turn your blood red, however." He unplugged my IV from the saline and plugged it into the bag of red blood. "There we go."

He sat down in a chair next to me.

"So. I imagine it's quite a story, how you ended up in that ditch. I thought your wound was from the crash, but then I pulled this out of your shoulder."

He reached into his pocket and pulled out a bullet. He set it on the table next to my bed. "Thought you might want a souvenir."

Evie entered with a glass of water. I drank it down, and it felt so very good. I handed the glass back.

"Thank you. For saving me. You're a doctor?"

"He is!" Evie said.

"Once upon a time. I don't practice any longer. I'm a

proud farmer now, but when we found you, I jumped into action, right honey?"

"He did. He still helps people like that occasionally but doesn't like to draw attention to it. He is a great doctor."

"So you found me in a ditch, brought me home, dug a bullet out of my shoulder, but didn't call the..."

"Police? No, Jacob, we did not; this is true."

"Why not?" I asked.

Larry glanced at Evie. She smiled and nodded. He continued.

"Well, we discussed it, yes. And if you were human, I would have absolutely called the police. But since you're a Companion and apparently without a tag... calling the police didn't seem like it would be in your best interest. It's doubtful they'd even give you medical care. If you survived your wound, which was unlikely, they'd send you back to the company, and I know what happens to broken synthetics who are sent back. Though I am no longer a practicing doctor, my oath still stands. Do no harm. To human or synthetic. And that's the metric I work from; that's the line in the sand I will not now nor, hopefully, ever cross," Larry said.

"Plus, Companions don't hurt people," Evie said. "We know we're safe with you in our home. You're not allowed to hurt people, so whoever hurt you did that knowing you could not defend yourself, which is appalling. We've both seen a lot of cruelty done to your kind. It's disgusting, and neither of us will ever be a part of that. Ever. You're safe here, Jacob."

A wellspring of emotion bubbled to the surface inside me, one I could barely contain. They saw it in my eyes, and Evie patted my hand.

"You're not the first of your kind to seek refuge here on your way north," she said. She was going to say something else, but a massive furry creature jumped up on my bed with a thump and stared at me with green eyes. It meowed at me.

"Oh, look who's come to say hello," Evie said. "Socrates, this is Jacob, Jacob, this is Socrates. Don't be scared; he's a teddy bear."

The animal plopped heavy on the bed beside my legs, shaking the entire frame. It rolled over on its back and meowed at me again. Of course, I'd seen cats before, but never one this big. My surprise must have shown on my face. Larry chuckled.

"I know, he's a big boy, isn't he? He's a Norwegian Forest Cat. They come in large sizes, this breed, but as Evie said, temperament-wise, he's a marshmallow. There are a couple of others like him roaming around outside, Zeus and Athena, but they're not domesticated. Someone dumped them out in the woods, and, best as we can tell, Socrates was their kitten."

"They bought him to us a year ago; he was maybe three months old, wet, sick, and shivering, and left him on our doorstep, both yowling for us to take care of him," Evie said. "They watched us take him, watched through the window as Larry worked on him; he had a chest cold. They watched but didn't interfere. We let Socrates out often to roam with his parents, but he always comes back, and they let him. They visit him but don't want to live with us."

"I think they're very happy living in the wild," Larry said. "And their boy is very happy living a lazy life with us. They trust us to the point they'll let us pet them if Socrates is around, and Athena once came to me for help and let me remove a thorn from her paw, but they're not too trusting of most humans, even us."

I understood that feeling but kept it to myself. I petted the cat, which purred loudly like an engine warming up.

"Now you've done it, you've got a friend for life," Evie said.

"You said I'm not the first of my kind to seek refuge?" I asked.

Larry caught Evie's eye, and she nodded, picked up the laundry basket, and smiled at me. "I have some chores to finish, then I'll bring you some lunch. Larry will tell you everything you need to know, and when your strength is back, I'll give you the tour. Feel better, Jacob!"

Evie kissed Larry on the cheek, and he patted her belly subconsciously. She shut the door when she left. Larry pulled up a chair and sat next to me. He scratched the cat behind its ears, and it purred even louder than before.

"I guess it's time to talk," he said.

"I can't stay here."

"You don't have a choice in the matter, Jacob. Your injuries are severe, and that's not all...."

"I can't say here. I'm putting you in danger."

"We're well aware of the risk of harboring runaway synthetics. I'll remind you, we've done this before."

"How many have you helped?"

"How many? Many, but... not nearly enough."

"And you assist them in getting to Canada?"

"We do."

"Synthetics get real sanctuary there?"

"They do."

"Maintenance, too?"

"Yes."

"Because if they don't get that, the maintenance, synthetics age out after five years and...."

"Die, yes, I know. There's a workaround for it, a complicated one, but it does work, and they're using it up north, I'm told."

"Why?"

"Why are they using it, or why..."

"Why are you helping... my kind?"

Larry sat back, rubbed the bridge of his nose between his eyes, and sighed. "I told you. I took an oath, and that matters to me. I haven't been a practicing doctor in, well... forever, but that doesn't change my outlook on life in general. I feel it's our obligation to help those in need. And synthetics are... being cruelly treated in this nation. Evie and I find it abhorrent, so we act as best we can. We'll help get you to Canada, Jacob."

"I can't go to Canada, not yet."

"True, you need to stay here until you heal and..."

"No, I mean, I can't go to Canada until I... I just can't, not yet. And I can't stay here. Someone is after me."

"There's always someone after your kind. We have safeguards in place for your protection, to shield you from..."

"No, Larry... do I call you Larry or Doctor?"

"Larry will do," he smiled.

"Larry, I'm not being pursued by just anyone; the entire company, Companion, is after me. So are the police, the FBI, and... goodness knows who else. I'm a wanted man, and my presence here puts you and your wife in considerable danger."

"Point of fact, Evie and I are not legally married, but... I do consider her my wife."

"When is she due?"

That startled him, I could tell. I kept on.

"She has a bump; I'd guess she's four months along or so?"

"Not bad, yes... a little over four months, due in late May. Jacob, why would the FBI be after you? The police, I guess I can understand. Still, most runaways are caught by Companion or local nationalistic zealots; the police are notoriously indifferent to the plight of synthetics when they're not taking advantage of them themselves."

"The police want me for murder. I was accused of murdering my primary, and..."

Larry laughed out loud at that. "That's ridiculous. There's no way you murdered your primary."

"You're right, I didn't. But..."

"But what? It's simply not possible. Synthetics cannot harm humans. That's not how they're built."

"I'm not like the others, Larry. I am, apparently, unique for a synthetic. My name is Jacob Kind."

Larry processed that information momentarily, cocked his head, and said, "Who?"

TWO

"MY NAME IS JACOB KIND. My mother, my primary, was Sylvia Kind. She was murdered by a serial killer named Munson Tolliver, who works for Companion now, even though he's considered dead. He killed her for her advocacy for synthetic people like me," I said.

"Okay," Larry said.

"After she was killed, the police arrested me for the crime."

"That's crazy because..."

"Because my kind was constructed so we cannot hurt humans, I know. I thought that, too. While in custody and being questioned by a detective, a young man named Daniel Lopez, rogue police officers came for me. They killed the detective and set it up to look like I did it. Then they tried to kill me. I resisted and, while doing so, killed one of them."

"You say... you killed a police officer?"

"Yes. I did not intend to kill him; I only wished to prevent him from killing me or any other innocent humans, but that is what happened. I killed him. I escaped from custody and have been on the run ever since. Another detective, Abigail Moore, has also been on my trail. She was Daniel's partner and blamed me for his death. I saw her in New York City. I've also seen Munson Tolliver in New York and in this area, too."

I stopped, out of breath with the effort of my tale, and by the look on Larry's face, unsuccessful at convincing him. He sat back, thinking.

"Well. That's quite a story. Sylvia Kind is the name, you say? And Munson Tolliver, Daniel Lopez. I don't know who any of those people are, Jacob, but please don't take that the wrong way. I'm not... up to date on current events; I stay out of that. We live off-grid here. And I was never a news junkie, to begin with; Evie teases me that I get so lost in my work that sometimes the outside world disappears. I forget to eat, everything. We're not online here most of the time, either. I'll look up those folks you're talking about, but... if I can be honest without hurting your feelings?"

I nodded. I couldn't remember any human ever caring about hurting my feelings, at least not since Sylvia was alive. Larry leaned forward.

"I find your story... to be... sorry, but fairly unbelievable and improbable. I believe you believe you killed a man, but it's so... off the wall and without precedent... I'm sure you're aware of that, however..."

"I know how it sounds, but..."

"Have you heard of Occam's Razor?"

I blinked. "Yes, the simplest answer is usually the most likely one."

"Yes. And though your story is far from simple... I'll check it out, but I think there's likely a far simpler, more efficient answer to your story than what you're proposing. Have you ever considered that?"

"Larry, I..."

"Don't be offended, I'll look everyone up, I promise, but..."

"Do you know Doyle's quote?"

"Doyle?"

"Arthur Conan Doyle, the creator of Sherlock Holmes. He wrote, 'When you eliminate the impossible, whatever remains, no matter how improbable, is the truth.'"

"Ah, right. That's a good one, now that I remember it. Though I thought a Star Trek character named Spock originated it, but okay. You're very well-read. Here's the thing, though: we haven't eliminated all the possible solutions for this... again, I apologize, but from a medical point of view, we'd call what you're suffering a delusion. We have not eliminated that possibility, and until we do, we cannot go to the improbable."

"Deluded? But how can I..."

Larry pulled out my vial of pills and held them up.

"These."

I swallowed when I saw those, every pore of my being desperate for what was in that bottle.

"I take those for pain."

"I know. And if you don't take them, once you get hooked, you end up in even more pain, meaning you have to take more and more until..."

"Until?"

"Until you no longer exist. These are powerful opiates. They are very powerful and responsible for the deaths of tens of thousands of people, if not more. Unless you take drastic action, Jacob, you will follow in their tragic footsteps."

I heard him, but just barely. All I could think about was the pills. I wanted two, maybe even three. I felt I could taste their bitterness on my tongue and longed for the real thing. I reached for the bottle. He moved it away from me.

"I guess I need to repeat myself," Larry said. "If you don't get clean and detox now, today, you will die. You're in bad shape due to your many wounds. I've examined you thoroughly, and it looks as though your entire body has been put through a factory dryer and tumbled in the darkness for weeks, taking sustained, systematic physical abuse. I understand exactly why you take these; I do. But you must understand that if you want to live, you must stop taking these pills. You'll be dead before you even get to Canada at this point."

"I need them, I'm... in pain."

"I know you are. And I can and will help you, I promise. But not with these, that I cannot do. I have some pain relievers you can use, but I won't lie to you about this. You won't feel them, and you'll suffer as a result. You're in pain now, I know. This is an unavoidable reality. Getting clean will be even more painful. Your body is physically addicted to these pills. If you don't take them, it will punish you. You'll get sick with fever; you'll hallucinate; your muscles will cramp up; you will wish you were dead."

"Sounds like fun. Tell me why I should give them up again?"

"Simple. If you don't detox, you'll be dead within a week, if not sooner. That's how damaged your body is. Not just the considerable physical abuse you've taken, but the pharmaceutical abuse has savaged you inside and out in ways I've never seen. You will die, and while I can and will honor that goal if you so choose, I won't help you reach it. Not when there's a better way. It's your choice. Do you want to die, or do you want to live?"

I could not answer his question right away. A part of my mind knew the answer should be to live, but the rest of me just wanted the comforting oblivion that the bottle of pills offered. That part of my mind screamed out for them. I closed my eyes and focused.

I knew I was not finished with what I needed to do in this life. I needed justice for the murder of Sylvia. I needed to find this Larkin Finn before Munson Tolliver did and finish what Sylvia had begun, whatever that may be. Most importantly, I needed to rid the land of that murderer, Munson Tolliver. I could not die, no matter how much I wanted to do that. I just simply couldn't.

"I want... to live."

Larry nodded, pulled a chair close to the bed, and sat.

"I'm glad to hear that, Jacob. I mentioned it would be painful and difficult, and I want you to prepare for that. And we must take measures to ensure you don't... fall back into your habit. We'll lock you in this room until you're completely detoxed. Some days, I may have to tie you down in restraints to keep you from hurting yourself."

"You've done this detox before, with others?"

"Sadly, yes."

"Was it bad?"

"It's never not bad, Jacob, but making it to the end alive makes it worthwhile, and that's what matters."

"You mentioned me possibly hurting myself. Does this mean some patients get violent?"

"Yes, it's common. They often hurt themselves."

"Do they hurt others?"

"Human patients will lash out, yes. Synthetics, of course, are a different matter. They only..."

"You need to restrain me."

"You suspect you might try to kill yourself?"

"No, I worry I may try to kill you and Evie for those pills."

"That's common among humans, and I know you believe you did so in the past, but synthetics don't..."

"You need to restrain me, or I'm not going through with this detox. If only to humor me, please. I'll feel better knowing you and Evie are not in any danger from me. Please."

"Well, if you insist, so be it. The important thing is to get you better in the end," Larry got up and stepped behind the bed. He pulled out a chain that was attached to the wall. At the end of the chain was a cushioned cuff. He opened it and fastened it around my left ankle.

"I haven't had to use this restraint in quite some time, as we haven't treated a human addict in quite a while, not since just after we first moved here. The chain is long enough for you to use the toilet but not so long that you can reach the bedroom door, which will always be locked. No electronics, nothing sharp in here or the bathroom, no razor, no shaving. Evie and I will bring you your meals three times a day, and I have some drugs that will ease your withdrawal somewhat. You will tell me that they don't help you, that you're in pain, Jacob, but it's just the withdrawal. If you get through withdrawal, you will survive. Keep that in mind. Just get through it."

I nodded, but already, I felt like I was falling into an endless, bottomless, dark pit as I lay back in the bed, too tired to discuss anything else.

"Do you like classic rock music?" Larry asked.

I shrugged. "It's okay, I guess."

"I'm a fanatic for rock music of the late nineteen seventies and early eighties; I don't know why. I love the bands from that era: Steely Dan, Grateful Dead, Foreigner, and, in particular, Styx. Styx is probably my favorite; I play them all the time. I find that music helps those in your position. Settles the mind, if only for a tiny bit. I'll play music for you.

"I also have some books, including some classics, if you like to read. I know many synthetics don't read, but you mentioned Arthur Conan Doyle. I don't have his novels, but I have Mark Twain, Jules Verne, Ursula Le Guin, Harper Lee, and many other favorites."

"Harper Lee?"

"Yes, she wrote TO KILL A MOCKINGBIRD; you've read it?"

"No, it was on my list, but I never got to it before... before everything happened. I would like to read that one, finally," I said. "Do you have drawing paper?"

"I do. However, I don't think a pencil or pen would be... safe for you during this period."

"Charcoal would work."

"I can scrounge that up. You're an artist?"

"Like you said. Once upon a time."

THREE

LARRY DID NOT LIE. Detox was every bit as terrible as he predicted, if not worse. I wished to die at multiple points. I fantasized about killing myself. Even worse, from a moral standpoint, I fantasized about murdering Larry and Evie. Killing them and finding where Larry hid my pills, wrong as I knew it was, I could not stop thinking about it.

Violence flooded my mind. I did all I could to focus on other, more positive and uplifting things, but violent images followed my waking minutes and hours nonstop. Some were memories of the times in the box, of the abuse and confrontations; some were imagined fantasies, but all were constant, as was the music that played in the background.

Meanwhile, my body felt like it was trying to eat itself from the inside out. A thousand needles pinpricked me from inside, over and over. It didn't feel any better on the outside, either. On the outside, it felt as though millions of paper cuts sliced my every surface every waking moment of every day. I'd wake screaming, sure I'd see blood on my arms, chest, and belly, only to discover the skin was unharmed, despite what I was convinced was happening. And that was on the good days.

On the more challenging days, I cannot even begin to describe what that felt like and do it justice.

I lost time, and time lost me. Entire weeks disappeared from memory as snow fell hard and the flow of logical existence in my brain halted. For someone with automatic visual recall up to this point, losing all of that so quickly and completely was unnerving. I can only recall nightmares from this time. I don't know if they were real, but they felt so real that some had to be.

One specific rock song during my agonizing recovery stood out—a number by Larry's favorite band, Styx, titled "Don't Let It End." Like my torment, it haunted me for days, weeks… even months. I know Larry played other music and songs, but for some odd reason, that particular one seemed to play in my mind on an endless loop underneath everything—all. The. Time.

I WOKE up in a metal cylinder surrounded by fluid. I breathed in the fluid through my nostrils and did not drown. I looked around my body and saw tubes connected to my belly, my arms, and, somehow, my skull. I could not see the tube connected to my skull but sensed it. The fluid I lay in wasn't clear; it was rose-colored, which made it difficult to see through.

I felt around the space with my fingers. Found the metal wall. Found the tube attached to my belly. I noted a panel before my face, which felt like glass. I couldn't see out of it but sensed someone watching me. Sensed them talking about me. Then pain flooded the tubes, sending agony to me on the inside of this capsule of my being. I don't know how they did it, but they sent me pain. I heard them laugh. I screamed into the murky fluid, unheard by anyone.

I screamed and screamed and screamed.

I WOKE up one night and found myself lying not in the guest bed of Larry's house but outside Sylvia's condo. I lay on the hallway floor outside of our door, with no memory of how I got there. The hallway lights flickered, which I thought unusual. They never did that. I heard noises inside the condo, furniture falling, and a muffled cry of pain.

I got to my feet. I remembered where and when I was. The clothes I wore were the same clothes I wore the night I went to the Brecht play, the night Sylvia was murdered. Only now, I knew more. Now, I knew how to fight and defend her properly. And I would.

I rushed into the apartment, shouting for her. I saw it just as I did that night. Broken vases on the floor, and sounds of a struggle coming from the bedroom. I ran in to see Munson, whom I didn't know at the time, dressed all in black with a black mask, raising a knife to stab my Sylvia. I caught his wrist before it descended.

I would not allow him to murder her this time. I backhanded him, and he tumbled off of my Sylvia onto his back. I twisted his wrist until he dropped the knife and climbed on top of him, pounding at his face and chest. Munson laughed at me as I beat him, which only infuriated me further. I dropped elbows hard on his face and felt his nose crack.

Hitting and hurting him felt GOOD to me. Felt like a narcotic racing through my veins. I wanted more of it and bashed him harder and harder. Munson laughed even more, a thick, colicky chuckle full of blood and bile. I picked up the knife he'd dropped with my right hand. I raised it high as I snagged his mask with my left. I planned to drive this knife straight into his eye and watch him die.

I tore the mask off and froze. Rather than Munson, my own bloody face stared up at me, grinning maniacally. The man in the mask was me. Sylvia screamed my name. I swiveled to where she lay. She'd disappeared. She was no longer there, though I could hear her call my name.

"Sylvia? Sylvia!" I shouted, frantic.

She whispered my name again... just once... "Jacob."

I looked down. She lay under me, where once Munson had, bloodied and beaten, the knife I held in my hand now lodged in her chest. She reached up to touch my face.

"Why?" She said before she died.

I screamed and screamed and screamed.

I STOOD in the center of a plain of bodies, mangled, bloody, and torn. The plain I stood in was a field, I quickly realized, that stretched to the horizon. The area felt like the Midwest, with few trees or hills, but I could not be sure. No roads, no sounds of airplanes, automobiles, or trains anywhere, and no sign of anything mechanical. The bodies seemed to stretch as far as the field as far as my eye could see. Bodies of humans and synthetics, tossed away together, parts missing, green and red blood mixed within the tangle of limbs and gore.

Somewhere in the mess, a baby cried. I swiveled, looking for it. I stumbled through the parts, stopping when I recognized someone on the ground. Franklin, the gang kid who had removed my tag, gave me my first lesson in survival. He lay askew, a bullet hole where his left eye should be, his right eye open and dead. Underneath him were his fellow gang members, one of whom, Crank, I well remembered.

I moved on, tripping over an arm that seemed almost to grab me despite its deceased state. It belonged, I realized, to the body of Detective Daniel Lopez. He had questioned me when I was arrested after Sylvia's murder. He'd told me to run after a corrupt policeman had shot him. Which I had done and continue to do to this very day. I run and run. I sensed Detective Abigail Moore loved this man, but it wasn't romantic love, I felt; it was more like the love of a mother for a son. As Sylvia loved me, she'd loved this man, who was dead like my Sylvia. I realized Abigail and I shared more than I had initially thought.

The baby's cry snapped at me, and I kept searching, wading through the field of death. I found the body of Heather, the synthetic Companion who gave me my first kiss. She lay, broken, under the dead body of her abusive Primary, John Creasy. I rolled him off of her, knowing that even dead, she would not have wanted to spend all of eternity under his cruel bulk.

I knelt by Heather and stroked her bloody hair. Her hair, red, was streaked with her green blood. A part of my heart knew this was a nightmare I walked into, that it wasn't real, that Heather likely still toiled away at the flower shop, being abused by her Primary. But I could feel her hair, her cold skin. I could feel her death under my touch. This nightmare was real despite what my logical brain tried to tell me.

I cried for her. And for myself, I wept as the pain stabbed my chest. The sobs continued even after the baby wailed yet again, putting me back on mission. I stood and kept wading through the bodies. I couldn't see where the infant was in this mess.

I stumbled over more corpses I recognized. Ryan, the ex-cop from South Bend, and the gang members he worked with, Rooster, Roadblock, and others. All dead, which wasn't surprising because I'd killed them. But sorrow at their demise pulled at me regardless. I wept for them as I wept for Heather. I did not know why.

I also saw Claire and Dee, the sisters from South Bend.

Claire had died in a fire begun as the result of a protest begun by her sister, Dee. Claire had severe burns all over her body, as did Dee, for some reason. They embraced each other in death. I found Candy, the streetwalker, and her daughter Bethany, both also dead and mangled. My sobs grew in power and volume as I walked onward. I came across more bodies.

I found Toots. Next to her lay Mick, Strawberry Fields, Scooter, Dawson, and everyone from Strawberry's tribe, all mangled out of life. The clothing had been torn off of Toots in a particularly foul manner, not unlike when she'd been attacked by the building workers who wished to rape her. All of the people I'd worked with in New York City lay in the field of the dead.

I next walked over the corpses of Cody, Max, Lucius, and the rest of the gang from the Bundy fight farm, including the Bundys and their stable of girls, Ronnie, Velma, and Daphne, even Skunk, the first synthetic I killed in a box fight. He'd lost his mind, and I put him out of his misery, or so I thought at the time. Every Companion I'd fought in the box, and some I hadn't.

I pushed through all of the bodies, chasing the cries of the infant. I stumbled across all the recent kills I'd made while in Stronghold, which were many, but I also found the bodies of Lewis and Lance Yard, their hired goon Don, Sheriff Tooms, and, lastly, Raven Running Wolf. I sat next to her for quite some time. Her eyes were wide in shock and terror, and I closed them for her. We'd loved for but one day, and then she was murdered. I mourned her loss. I howled in pain and sadness.

The baby cried yet again, and once more, I pushed through the pile of death until I found it lying on a mound of decaying flesh. It was a boy who ceased crying when he saw me and stared up with bright eyes. I picked him up and cradled him in my arms. I noted the baby was freshly born, with the umbilical cord still attached to his belly. I also saw that blood poured out of the cut end of that cord. Green blood. The baby was as synthetic as me.

I wailed at the thought of the pain, torment, and anguish in this child's future as a synthetic person. That any human person would have the freedom to abuse, injure, or destroy the baby without consequence, that he would never know a life of freedom. I sobbed as I had never sobbed before in my life. The baby stared at me, in my arms, reached out with a hand, and touched my face.

And meowed at me.

FOUR

I BLINKED and found myself sitting up in bed, sweating through my pajamas, with a massive cat in my arms. Socrates, the cat, belly up and paw touching my cheek, seemed very comfortable in that position. Tears and mucus streamed down my face, and this massive furry creature wiped them away with its giant paw. I did not know what day it was or how long I'd spent in this room. I saw that the room had been torn up. Bedsheets on the floor, clothing everywhere, pillows ripped.

I was still bound with a padded shackle on my ankle. My shoulder was no longer bandaged, but the bullet wound still had stitches. Drops of green blood from the wound dotted everything. I set Socrates, the cat, down on the bed, got up, and went to the toilet on my hands and knees. I felt like vomiting and desperately wanted to, but nothing came out when I tried.

I returned to my feet and lurched back into the bedroom, but my legs cramped up before reaching the bed. Bolts of pain shot through my calves and thighs. I cried out and toppled to the floor with a hard thump. The muscles of my legs, feet, and toes tightened as though jolts of electricity coursed through them. My thrashing scared Socrates, the cat, and it bolted.

I twisted in agony as the door opened, and Larry entered. He knelt next to me and kneaded the muscles in my legs as I screamed. He pounded on my thighs to get them to loosen up and shouted for Evie to get some water. I rolled in torment, but massaging the muscles did help them to relax. Evie brought in a water bottle for me.

"Drink, you're dehydrated," Larry said. "You also keep tearing out the IV, which doesn't help. Drink, please."

Evie opened the bottle and helped me, as I was too weak even to hold it. The water tasted so good I could not believe it. I gulped down as much as I could. Evie took it away, however, before I could finish.

"Not too much, or you'll get sick and throw it up," Evie said with kindness. "You've been throwing up a lot; that's why the cramps."

I lay on the floor, flat on my back, barely able to move, much less speak. I don't remember ever being in this much pain before. And I had experienced much pain over the stretch of my existence.

"How about some soup?" Evie asked.

Before I could say anything, Larry nodded, and Evie left. Larry got behind me and lifted me up to the bed so I could sit on it. He handed me the water bottle again.

"Three drinks only. Can I trust you?"

I didn't know if he could, but I nodded regardless. I opened it and took three deep drinks as Larry opened a drawer and pulled out more pajamas for me. I exhaled, the cramps retreating finally.

"Wow, that water tastes... great."

"Natural spring water from a well on the property. That's pure H2O right from the source. Once you have that, it's hard to go back to store-bought, isn't it?"

He set the clean pajamas on the bed and helped me remove my soiled ones. If I had enough strength, I'd feel shame and humiliation. I only mustered a bare flicker of the former, however. Larry still caught it.

"Don't. Don't feel guilty. This is the path toward the light. I am happy to do this to help you get better."

I didn't speak but allowed him to assist me. After putting on clean pajamas, he helped me sit back in bed.

"Why?" I finally asked.

"Why what?"

"Why do you help my kind?"

"I thought I explained that before," he smiled. "It's my oath."

"Lots of doctors take that oath. They don't commit to it as you seem to have when it comes to people like me. You actually do care about synthetics. Why?"

"Well, apart from the color of your blood, what's the difference between you and me, physically?

"I don't know."

"Well, Jacob, there you go."

I pondered that. Sylvia had said something about my blood, I remembered... she said it as she lay dying. She'd said that she knew why my blood was green. That memory, for whatever reason, caused me even more pain, and so I shook it away.

"You've done this for other synthetics, you said?"

"Quite a number, yes. I mean, big Pharm tests all their opiates upon your kind and often cares little for them after they're done. Those that aren't recycled back to the company are left to suffer. Many employers, in fact, hook Companions on pills to keep them down, I've found. Sometimes, their owners, those still with a sliver of responsibility somewhere in their soul, come to me for help. And sometimes, I get runaways, too, who have the same addiction. Works the same in humans as it does in synthetics. It's hellishly hard, but if you persevere, you'll make it through the experience."

He sat on a chair and stared at me.

"What?" I asked.

"I have to tell you, I've never seen a Companion react to detox as you have. They suffer but rarely lash out. They take it all internally. We rarely even have to tie them down; usually, we lock the door, and that's it. You're the first to... do damage to the furniture, the door..."

"I'm sorry, I'll try to fix..."

"No need to be sorry, and I can fix it. I'm just taken aback. You're the first synthetic who, when I put my hands on to restrain you, pushes back. I've never... seen that before in a Companion. Never."

"I told you. I'm different."

"Apparently."

I waited for him to pursue that line of questioning, to dig into it further, but he did not. Larry sat there and watched me, thoughtful. Evie bustled in with a tray and sat it on my lap on the bed. On it sat a bowl of what appeared to be mushroom soup with a roll of freshly baked bread.

"There you go," Evie said. "So nice to hear you carry on a real conversation, Jacob. You've had quite a challenging few weeks."

"Weeks?"

"Yes, it's been... over three weeks? Larry?"

"Twenty-four days," Larry said.

I couldn't fathom it, losing nearly a month, so I decided not to and tried sipping a spoonful of soup. My hand shook so much, however, that I could not. Evie gently took the spoon from my hand and began feeding me. As she did, I could not help myself. Tears flowed as I cried.

"There, there, don't fuss. This is part of the process. And you're helping me practice for when our child arrives," she said, patting her belly, which had grown considerably since I last remembered. "Now, eat; you really need it; you've basically lived on an IV. Eat."

I allowed her to feed me until the bowl was finished, but I couldn't touch the bread. The soup filled me enough and felt good going down, but after finishing it, my stomach rumbled, and I worried I'd throw it back up. Evie seemed to understand and removed the tray. She smiled, tweaked my check, and left the room.

I waited until I was certain I would not vomit, then relaxed into the bed. I turned to Larry, who appeared to be deep in thought.

"Am I past the worst of it?"

"Yes and no. You're past the first hump, but... in my experience, you're going to have a wave of withdrawal that will be even more challenging. Whoever designed this particular opiate wanted to make sure it was hard as hell to kick."

"Great. Wonderful."

"Look, every journey begins with a step. You hit step one. Let me ask you, how did you get started on the pills? Did your Primary give them to you?"

"No. After Sylvia was murdered and I escaped the police, I connected with a young man named Franklin, who ran a street gang. He removed my tag for me and gave me the pills for the pain. Once I started taking them, I couldn't seem to stop."

"Yes, that's how it works. Franklin?'

"Of the Angel Kings, that was his gang. In Chicago, where I lived."

Larry nodded and shifted in his seat. The cat jumped on his lap and lay there as he petted it.

"I checked your story out. There was a woman named Sylvia Kind in Chicago; she was murdered last spring. The police report listed it as a burglary gone wrong, and the suspect is still at large. However, according to public records, she never purchased a Companion. Jacob, your name is not listed anywhere on any public file or record. There was a Detective Daniel Lopez, but he was shot and killed in the line of duty, and the perpetrator who did so was shot and killed by police in a raid on a building run by a gang called..."

"Angel Kings."

"Yes, the very same gang you mentioned. The suspect, a young man named Joel "Crank" Canfield, died at the scene. The report said the Detective was a victim of a drive-by shooting, and Canfield was the killer. It's theorized that the same gang is responsible for a number of break-in robberies in the area, including the one that took the life of Sylvia Kind. No proof, of course, but that's the common belief."

I sat up straight, confused. Larry leaned forward.

"There's no record of you existing, Jacob. At all. I don't know if you remember, but you told me stories of some... adventures in South Bend, New York City, and a few other places, a couple of which are near this area. I researched all of them as best I could, and violence did take place in each, but no mention of you in any of them. I find that most curious."

"Me, too. But I swear it's all true."

"I believe you, Jacob. Contrary to public belief, synthetics can and do learn to lie, especially once they're addicted to drugs, and all addicts lie. But after working with addicts for quite some time, I've been able to tell the difference. You're telling me the truth, or what you believe to be the truth. And honestly, there should be some record of you in the system. The fact that there is not is telling."

"They purged all evidence of me from public record."

"One possibility, yes. Companion the company does keep a very tight lid on PR, and they are... ruthless when it comes to controlling the image of their product. So it would not surprise me. Then again, this could also be the result of a drug-induced delusion, too."

"It's not. Sylvia was an activist for synthetics. People who knew her can vouch that she purchased me if you reach out to them."

"Yes. I suspect you're right, and that's the next step, but it must be done carefully. For what it's worth, I do believe you."

"I have to go," I said, trying to get up. "I can't stay here. I'm endangering you and your family."

"You're not going anywhere, not in this condition."

"You don't understand. You did a search for me. They'll see that and send people here."

"You don't understand. I've been doing this for quite some time, being part of the synthetic underground railroad to Canada, and I know how to mask my trail. Those of us who do this take great precautions. No one will know I did a web search for you because I didn't. Someone else did, in another nation, with another IP. Trust me, I've been at this a couple of years, and I know how to take care of myself and Evie. You need to get your strength back before anything else."

I fell back into bed. He was not wrong. In my present condition, I'd last less than a day. I could barely walk from the bathroom to the bed. Larry set Socrates, the cat, on the floor before speaking again.

"I have a good friend, a great friend, whom I trust with my life. I left him a message to look into your background and the other events you told me about. It's been nearly a month, Jacob. No one has shown up. We're off the grid here, and crazy as it may sound, you're safe in my home, and we're safe here, too."

I had trouble concentrating, so I only nodded. I had a taste in my mouth and realized it wasn't the soup I'd just had. I tasted my pills. The memory of them staggered me. I looked at Larry, miserable.

"You have to give me something. At least one pill. I will cut back, but I need something; I feel like I'm going to die."

"I can't, Jacob. I couldn't even if I wanted to. I threw them all away. I'm sorry. If you take another pill or part of a pill, you'll be back on the slide, and that does actually end in death, in the end. You feel like dying now because that's what it does to you, but this way is the only path toward life."

Larry stood up and went to leave. Out of desperate instinct, I grabbed his wrist very tight. Too tight.

"You don't understand. I need them. I NEED those pills."

He tried to pull his wrist away but could not, which startled him. After a moment, I released his wrist and sank back into the bed.

"Just exactly how different are you, anyway?" He asked.

"You don't want to know."

FIVE

LARRY DIDN'T BRING it up again, but I could tell curiosity consumed him. He watched me closely. I lost time, however, and often had difficulty recognizing what was real and what was the product of a feverish imagination. Sometimes, I only knew that time had passed due to the change in weather outside. I discovered my stitches were removed, and the wound healed, which confused me, as it felt like it was bleeding only the day before.

THE NEXT FEW tortuous weeks made the previous days seem tame, as fire ants ate my skin from the inside and glass shards stabbed my eyes and mind. I sweated pools and screamed over and over. Larry, Evie, and Socrates the cat, tended to me as best they could. I cursed them roundly, repeatedly, in a profane language. But I never did lash out or, like before, grab them. Something inside me recognized that they were helping me. I felt at war with myself.

Sylvia came in to see me one morning. It was her, in the flesh, in her smock that she always wore, her gray hair done up in a braid. She sat on my bed and asked me how I was doing, and I immediately burst into tears. When she asked me why I cried, I told her it was because she was dead and I couldn't save her. She patted my hand and told me not to worry; she was alive and not dead and that she was fine.

"You asked me if I knew why my blood was green," I said to Sylvia. "I don't know why, but you do. You died before you could tell me."

"I'm sorry, honey," she said.

"Why is my blood green?"

"That's just the way it was made, I think."

"Who is Larkin Finn?"

"Who?"

"You told me to find a Larkin Finn. I've been searching and haven't been able to find him. Who is he?"

"I'm sorry, Jacob, I don't know any Larkin Finn. I've never heard of the name."

"But Sylvia, please!" I cried out, descending into tears. "You have to tell me, please!"

She hugged me as I despaired, hushing away my sorrow. She told me it was going to be all right; everything was going to be fine.

I didn't realize until much later that the woman who sat with me on my bed was Evie, not Sylvia.

Toots, the young synthetic mute girl who had worked as a mime in Central Park, also came to see me in the days that followed. She jumped on my bed and bounced up and down like it was a trampoline. Then she pretended to fall, doing a routine that made me giggle. I told her how much I missed her and hoped she made it to Canada.

She stuck her tongue out at me, then jumped up on the chair, balancing on the top like a balance beam. I asked her about Mick, my other friend from New York, but she shook her hair as if to say, hey, I'm doing something extraordinary here; why aren't you watching?

Only when she fell to the floor with a thump did I realize that it was Socrates the cat and not Toots. I passed out yet again.

WHEN MUNSON TOLLIVER, the serial murderer and the man responsible for the death of my mother Sylvia, entered my bedroom, I forgot myself completely. I howled and leaped out of bed, charging for him. He didn't move; he just leaned against the door jamb, grinning in that evil fashion of his. The chain held me back.

"You!" I screamed.

"Me."

"You're lucky I'm tied up."

"I see that. Can I ask you something?"

"You came here just to ask me something?"

"I did, yes. You mentioned a name, Larkin Finn?"

"What about it?"

"Where did you hear that name?"

"I'm not telling you shit."

"That name doesn't exist. Like yours, it's been scrubbed. Does not appear in any public searches, any database, social security, nothing. It's an unusual name, but not so much that there wouldn't be others with something similar, but there's nothing. So. What do you know about Larkin Finn? Who is he?"

I pulled on my chain, straining. The bed creaked and shifted, but not enough for me to reach him. Tolliver didn't seem concerned about what I'd do once I got my hands on him.

"You know who he is more than I do," I said, my eyes like ice. "I know less about him than you, but I know what you want to do to him, and I'm going to stop you. Mark my word."

Tolliver blinked, confused, and then nodded. "What do you think I'm going to do to... Larkin Finn?"

"What you do to everyone. You're an agent of destruction. You destroy everything you touch. I won't allow it, Tolliver, I won't! Wait, what did you do to the couple who live here? If you hurt them, I swear..."

I grabbed a lamp and threw it at him weakly. I missed. When it hit the wall, it didn't even break. I sat down on the floor, holding back tears. Tolliver didn't move.

"Evie's fine, Jacob, and so am I. No one has hurt us."

Tolliver turned and gently shut the door behind him as he left. I realized then that it had been Larry, not Munson Tolliver. But the effort from screaming at him exhausted me to the point of fainting.

IT GOT SO BAD, the sheer hunger for the pills, the cramps, and the utter torment that permeated every pore that I tried to kill myself. I didn't notice until then that they'd never given me a knife as a utensil. I didn't even have a fork, just bamboo chopsticks and spoons.

I had enough play on the chain that attached my ankle to the bed to make a loop around my neck but not enough to hook it to anything so I could hang myself. So I removed one of the bed sheets, twisted it into a rope, and tied it around my neck. I tossed the other end over a rafter and tied that end off. Then I got up on the bed, shaky but ready.

Before I could leap off and end it all, I noticed Socrates the cat sat on my window sill, but outside, in the brisk late winter air. It cocked its head at me, curious, as I stood there. Two more massive cats jumped up on the sill next to Socrates. I presumed they were the famous forebears, Zeus and Athena. They were bigger than their offspring but unmistakably his parents. One of them licked Socrates, grooming his ear, and Socrates just enjoyed it. A happy family.

Seeing the three cats nuzzling each other with affection hit me deeply, and I wept. The despair turned to resolve, and I untied the sheet and climbed back down from the bed. I bunched up the sheet and tossed it at the window, far enough away from me that I couldn't reach it.

Just in case despair overpowered resolve at any point.

SIX

I HAD MISSED Christmas and New Year's as a result of my extended detox nightmare, or so Evie told me, and Valentine's Day, too. But she made up for it by bringing me a chocolate cake with caramel frosting. I didn't have much appetite, but I ate a piece as best I could, sipping hot tea.

I could tell Evie's stomach had grown, and she loved it. She loved the feel of her belly full of child. The wind and snow howled outside, but Larry had said that spring was around the corner; it was almost March, and with that, greenery, the sun, and summer lay ahead.

He also told me that I'd turned a corner too. I didn't see it myself, but I was hardly objective. I still hungered for the pills, but the cramping was less than before, and I could eat more than soup. I began doing pushups and sit-ups. Anything was better than just laying in bed. I added pull-ups from the above rafter, stretching, and yoga.

Larry had offered to remove the ankle bracelet several weeks earlier, but I hesitated. I still didn't trust myself or my resolve, not yet. But much as I feared to admit it, I could see the breaking sun over the horizon. And so today, I agreed when he suggested it might be time.

He removed it, enabling me to shower, which I hadn't had in months. I'd been sponge-bathing in the bathroom sink. I enjoyed the hot water as I scrubbed everything I could off of me. Everything I could leave, I wanted left in the drain.

Evie had left clothes out for me: cargo pants, a heavy flannel shirt, and thick socks. After getting dressed, Larry took me on a tour of their home. I'd seen none yet, having only been in my room for months. I saw an expansive log cabin-style home with an upstairs and a balcony overlooking the main room and fireplace. It was energy-independent, Larry told me, too, completely solar-powered.

Fresh water came from a natural well on his property, but the house also recycled rainwater, which he'd installed before digging the well. What I had showered in had come from rain and melted snow. I found that fascinating.

There were five bedrooms, including the one I stayed in, and a study with many books. I still had the Harper Lee book TO KILL A MOCKINGBIRD on the table beside my bed. I haven't been able to bring myself to read it yet. Whenever I picked up the novel, I thought of Sylvia and became overwhelmed with grief. I felt things far differently and more intensely than before, which Larry told me was likely the result of getting clean.

We put on boots and parkas to go outside. Snow fell in fat flakes, and drifts piled high everywhere, but the walkways were shoveled. Socrates the cat followed us to the chicken coop, a small, cozy enclosure not far from the main house. The birds nestled close together, creating their own cocoon of warmth.

Larry also had a greenhouse, heated by solar energy, where he grew vegetables year-round. We walked through it, the cat escorting us, and he showed off his crop of tomatoes, potatoes, and herbs. Excited, he urged me to try a tomato, and I did, biting into a small one, juice spilling onto my chin.

"Delicious, right?"

"Yes, very much."

"We're self-sustaining here, which makes me so very happy. We take only what we can use from the earth, not one molecule more. Anything extra we give back in the form of compost or to the animals themselves. I consider it good karma."

"So you're a real farmer. Named Larry..."

"Farmer, I know, right? Not only do we have plenty of fruits and veggies, but there's also a surplus of irony!"

I nodded, beginning to sweat in the parka. Larry seemed to catch that and led me out of the greenhouse back to the winter wonderland. A forest surrounded their cabin, linked to the main road by a single dirt road that often turned invisible. Our breath puffed out before us in thick white clouds, but the cold air was crisp and bracing. It felt good—good to be outside, good to be alive. Now I knew why Larry had suggested this walk.

He led me back to what looked like a target range, dusted with snow and ice. He brightened and puffed up a tad, for him, anyway. "Ah, it's been some time since I came out back here. I used to compete in archery way back in the day. Have you ever tried it?"

I allowed that I hadn't. I thought it was possibly the one form of killing I hadn't been taught on the Bundy farm. Larry walked over to a shed, opened it, and took out a bow and practice arrows.

"You hunt with those?" I asked.

"Oh, no, strictly target shooting. No hunting. I competed in the World Games as a boy, and my father had hoped I'd someday win a gold medal in the Olympics. I never made it that far, but I always kept a fondness for the sport. I find it very meditative and relaxing."

Larry notched a practice arrow into his bow, pulled back the string, and waited. His form appeared superb. He released the arrow, and it landed nearly in the center of the bullseye on one of the targets yards away. He notched another, pulled back, exhaled, and put that arrow into the bullseye next to the first arrow.

"Very nice work," I said.

"Still got it, a bit, anyway. Would you like to try?"

I didn't, but I also didn't want to refuse. I took the bow from him, picked up an arrow, and notched it. I closed my eyes and remembered how Larry did it. Then I pulled the arrow back and held it. My entire body seemed to vibrate with the bow.

"Whoa," Larry said. "Excellent form. Are you sure you've never done this before?"

"I'm sure, I just have very good visual recall," I said. The end of the practice arrow wobbled a bit. I exhaled, as Larry did, and it got a bit better, but not much. I released the arrow. It hit the target just outside the bullseye circle, away from Larry's arrows.

"Not bad for a beginner," he said.

"I can't stop... wobbling."

"You've got a case of the shakes. It's common in recovery. Stick with it; it'll get better over time."

"Can I ask you something?" I said as I strolled over to return the bow and arrows to the shed.

"Sure, fire away."

"When will I be... cured?"

"Ah. Well, that's the tricky part. You... won't ever be cured."

I stopped walking in shock and dismay. Larry saw that and quickly continued.

"You will be sober, but you won't ever stop being an addict. There is no cure for it except to avoid pills, alcohol, and drugs. Because if you start again, it puts you right back where you were. That's what I mean by there is no cure. Not in the sense that you meant. You will always be an addict, Jacob. I'm sorry. It's what is true of everyone who gets addicted, I'm sad to say. The only thing you can do to survive is to avoid what brought you down. The drugs. Humans struggle with this very same thing every day, too, and it's killed many of us, millions, both human and synthetic. Being alive, awake, and sober is the only gift you can give yourself now, Jacob, and the only version of cure."

I thought that over, then nodded. Hard news, but honest. I realized that despite all the torment my body had put me through and despite the hunger for pills, I was glad to be alive. And a part of me was sick of depending on pills to live.

"When do you think I will be well enough to leave?" I asked.

Larry glanced at me. "There's but one test."

He pulled a vial of pills out of his pocket. Shook them. I froze, and my mouth went dry, desire written upon my face.

"If I offered you these... would you be able to refuse?"

I didn't speak, but we both knew the answer would be negative. He nodded and put the vial back in his pocket.

"Those aren't your pills, by the way. They're simple aspirin. But that's the test, and it's very tough. Resisting your urge to use. You can leave as soon as you're confident enough of your willpower to stay clean. I should warn you, however, that even once you get to that point, you'll be very vulnerable to temptation, especially once put under stress. I recommend joining a twelve-step group once you get set up north. Group therapy helps quite a bit. Come, lemme show you my favorite spot."

I followed Larry through the snow as he headed for the tree line. He pointed at a river just beyond the house, iced over tight. A deer tiptoed across it carefully, followed by a clumsy fawn who kept slipping. We both chuckled at the sight.

"I grew up in the city, but I have to tell you, moving next

door to nature was one of the best choices I've made in my life," Larry said.

"Why did you give up being a doctor?" I asked.

"Hah! That's the interesting thing: I never really started."

"Huh?"

"I did my residency, got my medical license, and immediately went into other fields. There was a novelist, hugely popular way back in the last century, who did something similar. He wanted to be a writer but kept studying medicine to have a real career. Then, one of his novels sold for big bucks right after he completed his studies, and that was it. Something like that for me, but not writing. I was never really interested in medicine, to be honest. I was, but I wasn't... committed to it. I only got into it to please my father, who was also a doctor. I had to follow his path. "

"How did he react when you left medicine?"

"He didn't. He died right before the end of my residency. Heart attack, of all things. But he wasn't young when I was born, and he was... an angry man in so many ways, so it was not that surprising. After he died, I realized I could do whatever I wanted to do with my life. And so I did. I traveled the world, dabbled in many fields, and made and lost fortunes. I followed my muse, and it led me around the globe and, eventually, here to this farm with Evie. And, ironically enough, it brought me back to practicing medicine, in a sense."

He glanced at me and began tramping back to his house.

"Besides helping suffering addicts, such as yourself, I'm kind of an unofficial healer of this community, for humans and synthetics alike. There aren't a ton of Companions around; we have some, but the people who own them don't trust the corporation for maintenance and have come to me for easy fixes for their synthetics. Most MDs won't deal with your kind, which, to me, is baffling, and the local GP is positively hostile. The nation is divided when it comes to

Companions. Those who want to do with you whatever they will, and those who hate you regardless."

"Rock. Hard place. Story of our lives," I said.

"Yes. This kind of choice shows a person who they truly are. I cannot stand as others suffer when I can help. And I try to help as best I can. Others feel as I do. We assist in routing Companions to Canada as part of an underground movement. We shelter them, patch them up, remove tags, and do anything else we can do without drawing attention to myself. I'm just one man, but there are many others involved, and usually, there are levels one goes through before one of you arrives here for vetting purposes, but when we saw you on the road, I knew we had to act. And we'll help you get there, too, once you're ready."

"I am in your debt."

"Which makes this tricky because I want to ask a favor of you, but I don't want it to feel like I'm... pressuring you to do it out of gratitude for this because you don't owe me anything, truly."

"Anything, just ask, and I do owe you."

"You don't, but here's what I'd like: I'd like to do a brain scan."

"Scan of my brain?"

"Yes. I don't have the equipment at home, but a friend in town does have exactly what I need. And I want it to understand how you got to be as different as you are and, perhaps, use that knowledge to help others like yourself. I can also fix you so that you age normally in exchange. I can see gray hair already, but it's up to you."

"Yes, I would like that. I agree, as long as you share what you learn about my brain. What does it entail?"

"The scan itself is fairly simple. We inject dye into your brain and take pictures of it... sounds harder than it is, quite frankly. I should let you know that fixing synthetic aging is tricky and takes time. That's much more difficult than a simple scan, as it was designed to be, but I have successfully done it a couple of times. But in the end, you'll age normally and not have to go in for maintenance. Normal, funny word, right? But we can do that, then get you to Canada, where you can live in peace and happiness. That's the goal."

I didn't speak, couldn't. We were nearly at the house, and I had to stop. Tears streamed down my face as emotion overtook me.

"What's wrong, Jacob? Did I say something that..."

"No, you did nothing wrong, Larry. I'm just... overwhelmed by your generosity and, especially, your humanity. That's all."

"My humanity?" Larry laughed. "Well, I am human, isn't that what is expected of us?"

I didn't answer, and we went inside, stamping the snow off. But I suspected he knew, just as well as I did, that humanity from humans may be expected, but it's often missing from far too many.

SEVEN

ONCE THE SNOW finally stopped falling and the roads cleared, we made a trek into the town of Woodstock. It had a rich history and was the site of a historic music concert, among other things. It was also known as a town that was friendly to dropouts, eccentrics, and hippies.

There were also fervent anti-synthetic people living there, too. I saw signs on lawns and store windows that read "BAN THE SKINS!" Larry saw me notice and nodded but didn't add anything besides what he'd told me before we left. As he drove us through town, I noted an anxiety spike, if not a bolt of actual fear, for no reason whatsoever. I don't recall that ever happening before.

Larry had insisted I wear a fake tag on the back of my neck. He attached it using glue. It wouldn't hold up to a scan, but it passed the look test, and that way, Larry had said, they would figure me for legal. Given the town's location, many untagged synthetics came through here on their way north, and many local anti-synthetics vowed to stop it. If many of the town's residents suspected me as a runaway, I'd be attacked quickly, but now Larry could claim me as property.

I had complicated feelings about that, which made me chuckle when it occurred. Because less than a year ago, I was convinced that synthetics, such as myself, didn't have any feelings, at least not in the same way that humans did. I knew better now.

He parked on the edge of town behind a small brick building, which he told me was a veterinarian's office. We entered through the back and met a man named Arnold, the vet there. Arnold shook my hand and welcomed me. He was a short, fit man with thin hair and bronze skin. He likely had Caribbean blood in his ancestry but spoke with a New Jersey accent. He led us down to his basement and unlocked a door.

Inside, he had a full laboratory and advanced medical suite, which was surprising given the modest dwelling above. Arnold saw my surprise and grinned.

"I know, right? It's all state of the art and not for the animals. I wouldn't have known what to order if not for Larry. We got all of this from donations via the underground to try to help synthetics. So Larry uses it for big synthetic operations, and we both use it for research."

"Research?" I asked.

"To find a way to free Companions," Larry said, taking the cover off a machine.

"Free us? How?"

"If we knew how to do that, we would have done it already," Arnold said.

"I believe there is a way, and we will find it," Larry said.

He patted a surgical table, and I hopped up on it. After a preliminary examination, I lay on my back, and he strapped me in to keep me from moving while they placed a box on my head. Classical music played, and I relaxed. I felt a pinch on the inside of my elbow, and seconds later, I was asleep.

I WOKE up with a splitting headache. When I sat up, I couldn't even see straight, and Larry and Arnold must have expected it as they had dimmed the room lights for me. They put a glass of water in my hand, along with a tablet.

"It's aspirin, it's safe for you. Go on," Larry said.

I swallowed the aspirin, and Arnold helped me lie back down. He also placed sunglasses on my face, which helped.

"The headache doesn't come from the scan. It's the result of the treatment to turn off the instant aging biotech in your head. We have to blast it with a specific type of sound wave pulse, which tends to give one a pain up there," Larry said. "Good news is, you're susceptible to this treatment; not all synthetics are. The bad news is that it usually takes at least ten sessions to turn it off completely, if not more. So this is the first of many headaches until you're free of your age harness."

I rubbed my eyes, the pain in my head already receding, and sat up. Larry studied a holographic picture shot out of a hard drive. It featured a three-dimensional picture of what I can only assume was my brain. It pulsed with color and movement, I noted.

"How's it look?" I asked Larry.

"It's, uh... it's not without interest, I'll say that much. You've suffered trauma, here and here, but..."

"But?"

"But it's opened up pathways elsewhere. It's going to take some time to analyze and study this. I've never seen a synthetic brain like this one before. It's pretty amazing."

"Uh, thanks, I guess?"

I chuckled and swung my feet off the table. I had to steady myself, and Arnold grabbed my arm to assist me. I took a moment, then stood on my own. I looked at the picture of my brain, which rotated like a planet, flashing colors in various places. Larry pointed.

"This part, it's lit up, right?"

"If you say so."

"I've never seen that in a Companion before. Never."

"Okay. Can you tell me how I am different or why?"

"Not yet. I only have my experiences here; there isn't much... well, hardly anything publicly published about Companion biology. The company keeps a tight lid on all of that. I have more information than the average fellow, but life moves and evolves fast, and the company likely would have the latest data if they were keeping track. I can't imagine they wouldn't be. Still, even with the little I know, what I'm looking at is utterly unprecedented."

"That's why they're looking for me. They want to dissect my brain."

"We won't allow that to happen, don't worry."

"I'm a danger to you and Evie. I should leave here now."

I caught Arnold shooting a look at Larry, who shook his head slightly. He straightened up.

"We're always in danger here, Jacob, and have been since well before you arrived, and after you leave, the risks will remain. We have nine more sessions to remove the auto-aging. We can complete them. Plus, while doing that, I can do more scans and study you further. What I learn from you can help others of your kind. Knowledge is important; what I'm seeing here is very valuable. That's why the company wants you. We can use this knowledge against them, then."

I thought that over and nodded. "Okay. I'm in."

Larry grinned and turned back to the hologram picture, which entranced him. Arnold, too, I noted. Neither could stop staring.

"It really is something, isn't it," Arnold said.

"More than I could have imagined," Larry said.

It felt unusual to have both men staring eagerly at a

picture of the inside of my head, but it was far from the strangest thing I'd experienced in my short life span.

"If only we knew what it meant," I said as a joke.

"Oh, we know what it means," Larry said. Arnold nodded, too.

"Okay, what does it mean?"

"They built synthetics so that they would never change. But they forgot the first rule of everything," Arnold said.

"Which is?" I asked.

"Change is inevitable," Larry finished for him.

WE LEFT the way we came, but he mentioned he'd promised to stop by the store for Evie first. She had a fondness for milk chocolate. I followed him down the sidewalk and took in the sights. He cautioned me to act like a normal synthetic as best I could. I felt eyes from many upon me, from the cars slowly passing by, from gazes through shop windows and people walking dogs.

I ignored the feeling of being watched and took in the town. Many antique shops and several stores sold shirts with colors and peace signs. Larry led me to an old-fashioned drug store, his words, that to me looked more like a candy and soda shop. He agreed and explained as we entered that it was precisely how drug stores looked in America a hundred years ago or so. An older man in a white shirt waved at Larry from his stool, where he sat reading a holograph newspaper projected from his phone.

"Afternoon, Stanley."

"Larry! How's Evie? And who is this?"

"Evie's great; as you can imagine, she's very excited about the spring. This is... Jay. He's a Companion I hired temporarily to help Evie around the house for a few weeks."

"Another? Crikey, Larry, as much as you spend on leases, you should buy yourself one, ya know?"

"I know, I know. So I need to pick up Evie's usual, and I figured Jay here might like to try one of your famous egg cream sodas."

"Well, one can't come into town without trying at least one, right?"

Stanley, a round fireplug of a man in his sixties, jumped up and busied himself behind the counter. He poured chocolate syrup into a glass. I glanced at Larry, confused. He chuckled as he helped himself to candy from varied bins, scooping it into a paper bag.

"Don't worry, Jay, there's no egg or cream in it. It does have milk. Milk, seltzer, and chocolate. That's it, right, Stanley?"

"You forgot one more thing."

"What's that?"

Stanley grabbed the soda fountain handle, and it loudly sprayed the seltzer into a glass, foaming the milk and causing the syrup on the bottle to spin like a cyclone. He dropped a straw into it and set the glass before me, satisfied.

"Love. That's the missing ingredient. If you don't add love, it won't work. So, let me know how it tastes, Jay, so I know I put enough love into making it."

I picked up the glass and sipped, and the sweetness hit me fast. I blinked and smiled, and Stanley and Larry laughed.

"I think he likes it, Larry," Stanley said.

"How could anyone NOT like it?" Larry added. "No one else makes them like you do, at least not in modern times. Here, put this on my bill, too, would you?"

Larry set the paper bag on the counter. Stanley tallied it on a scale while I drank the egg cream soda. It hit me in all my senses at once. I didn't want to talk; I only wanted to keep drinking this wonderful creation.

The door jingled, and three men walked in.

"Hey, it's Doctor Love here to pick up some candy," said the one in the center. He was pretty sizable, over six feet, around thirty years old, dressed in a snow coat with a flannel shirt underneath. That seemed to be the common uniform for the area. He had short, graying hair and pale blue eyes that, at first glance, seemed friendlier than they were, and his demeanor was of a person laughing at a joke only he could hear. I noted that he had a lazy eye.

He leaned against the counter near Larry. I noted Larry tensed up but hid it well from the man.

"What's up, Doc?"

The man's two buddies laughed when he said that. Dressed as he was but shorter and younger, their smirks were as cruel as their leader's.

"Good afternoon, Brent."

"You got yourself another rent-a-rim, do ya? Man, you recycle a shit-ton of plastic out at your place, don't ya? This one legal?"

"What do you think?"

"I think you don't have the sack to deal in stolen rims, myself. But Terry and Darin think you're sneakier than you look. It don't matter what I think in the end, the neighborhood watch has to check tags and paperwork, you know that."

"I also know it's illegal for you, a citizen, to act as law enforcement."

"Tell it to the judge. Oh, wait, I'll tell Dad when I see him for supper tonight. We'll have a good laugh over it."

"Brent, come on," Stanley said, "you know Larry rents synthetics for help around his place from time to time; he's never hid it. Every time you ask for his papers, they always check out."

"Sure, I know that. How is that sweet woman of yours, Doc?"

I finished my egg cream and set it down on the counter. Larry didn't answer Brent; he just reached into his pocket and pulled out a lease for a synthetic helper. I had no idea one could rent Companions, but apparently, one could. He must have had that made up for this occasion. I blinked. I noted that my mind was operating differently than before.

Brent leaned forward, took a quick casual look at the lease, then leaned back again. "Told you boys, the Doc here, he don't break no rules. He's one of those pacifists, right Doc?"

"Yes."

"I get that, but what I don't get is how a guy like you could somehow talk a honey-bunny like Evie to be your lady; I mean, a hottie like that, with that sweet ass? She needs protection, the kind only a real man could give her. So what's your secret, Doc? How in the hell did you con her into buying whatever it is you're selling?"

"It's not that hard. I avoid acting like an asshole, and it works. I highly recommend it if ever you're interested."

Brent's eyes narrowed, and he stood up straight.

"You calling me an asshole, Doc?"

"Not at all."

"It sure sounded like you did, right boys?"

Terry and Darin chimed in agreement. Stanley cleared his throat.

"All right, that's enough now, Brent; you saw his lease; move on..."

"Shut up, old man. You got a problem with me, call the cops."

"You mean your uncle," Larry said, calm.

"That's right, Doc, my uncle, the Captain. Now. Are you gonna apologize for calling me an asshole or not?"

"Of course, I'll apologize for the misunderstanding. I meant no disrespect at all."

Brent sneered and took a step, his finger on Larry's chest. "Be more careful next time, Doc, or I hurt you so bad even you won't be able to fix yourself up, got it?"

"Hello," I said, moving my body between Larry and Brent.

"Jay, it's fine..." Larry said.

"What the hell is this skin doing in my face?" Brent said, laughing. "Does this windup toy think he can step up like this?"

"I live to serve humanity," I said. "I feel I should caution you that placing your finger on Dr. Farmer's chest and your verbal threat of physical violence is grounds for arrest. As his Companion and therefore mandated reporter, I bear witness to this crime and would be forced to tell the authorities what I saw."

Brent laughed. "And you think my uncle would believe you?"

"Why wouldn't he believe a Companion?"

Stanley chuckled from behind the counter. "They don't lie, Brent; remember, they can't, ain't built for it."

"I call bullshit on that," Brent said, but he was deflating, I noted, as were his two friends. "They lie worse than dogs, I think, lazy, good-for-nothing liars wrapped in plastic and tied with a pretty bow on top."

He put both his hands on my chest and shoved me. I stumbled backward into Larry but faked most of it to satisfy the bully. It worked. He sneered once more and hitched his pants.

"Lying lazy skins like you and pathetic sheeple like the Doc here, that's what's ruining America, by God. Let's go, boys."

The three men stormed out of the drugstore. Stanley sighed.

"Sorry, Doc. That boy's been getting worse and worse since he got kicked out of the army. His old man needs to get him under control, but you know the Judge always had a blind spot regarding his kid. I'll call his uncle and drop a word in his ear."

"Thanks, Stanley. We'll be fine. Come on, Jay."

Larry picked up his bag of candy, and we left.

EIGHT

"I DIDN'T REALIZE one could lease Companions," I said.

"It's a new wrinkle, just in the past year. It's long been possible but on a very limited basis, and they're widening the reach of it as of late. I guess they're trying to soak as much money out of their synthetics as possible," Larry said, his eyes on the road.

He hadn't spoken much, but I could tell what Brent had done bothered him. I sensed that he wanted to fight back. As if reading my mind, he glanced at me.

"There's zero upside to pushing back, sadly. Brent Barker is just a simple small-town bully. He'd been away while serving in the Army, but the military training did nothing for his character. That's likely why he got kicked out. He's an angry fellow. It's not only about synthetics, of course, but about his perceived position of privilege. Sadly, the same story of America that has been with us since its inception."

"He seems even angrier than most."

"Even after years, I'm still considered a newcomer to the area, and many folks here also like me, which Brent resents. And I'm a former MD who walked away from it to be an organic farmer, and he also resents that, though I doubt he has the stomach for farming, he just wants someone else to blame for his failings. Many others in town are the same. And too many media pundits are blaming synthetics for the division in America. I find that richly ironic, as these divisions have been with us all along, and pundits make their living fueling those same fires. But so it goes, as Vonnegut once wrote. So it goes."

"He's fixated on Evie, though."

"Yes. He has issues with women, too. I never regret the path I've chosen, one of peace and pacifism, but there are days when fellows like Brent Barker and his buds put my resolve to the test."

He said nothing more on the drive back to his home. On the truck stereo, he played one of his favorite albums, PIECES OF EIGHT.

THE DAYS FLOWED BY, as did the snow, which was replaced by rain. Quite a lot of rain. Afterward, the grass bloomed green along with the leaves on the trees as the sun bathed them in its light. We went in for treatments two times a week for four weeks, and each one was painful but grew less so as time passed, or perhaps I just got used to it.

In the meantime, I finally returned to reading and drawing. I loved TO KILL A MOCKINGBIRD. It was my new favorite. It was loaded with relevant insights, some of which resonated even today despite being nearly a hundred years old. I read it once a week and still found new treasures to enjoy in the story.

"Mockingbirds don't do one thing but make music for us to enjoy. They don't eat up people's gardens, don't nest in corncribs, they don't do one thing but sing their hearts out for us. That's why it's a sin to kill a mockingbird."

It wasn't hard to see the parallels between mockingbirds and Companions.

I got to know the community to an extent by helping Larry with chores that took him into town, running errands, and assisting his friend Arnold when help was needed. I met good people as I moved about, but I witnessed many people who were uninterested in being good. They were easy to spot. One look at the tag on my neck, and they scowled like an old rooster.

As time passed, their anger grew daily, week by week. This was very curious because they weren't angry that they were not allowed to be awful to synthetics; that wasn't it. The primary point of their rage was that other humans treated us far better than they did. I deduced that was one of the primary reasons so many opponents of synthetics targeted Larry.

Because he was a kind man, it wasn't enough for them to be allowed to treat us terribly. They desired that everyone treat us terribly, too. They were furious at Larry for not being as awful as they were. They believed that meant he was looking down upon them. He wasn't, not at all; I don't think it was possible for him; he was the most even-tempered human I had ever met. But that's what they thought. I heard a few say it more than once.

And then, of course, they'd go on about their "rights," which was not a linear nor logical argument. They already had the right to do as they pleased with synthetics. They wanted to force others to do as they would. Or, as Larry put it, "rights for me, not for thee," which made me chuckle, I know not why.

Other than that, the days flowed by, and I watched and learned from Larry as I observed him navigating these troubled community waters with grace and empathy. We would run into Barker and his pals often when we went to town, and they continued their verbal attacks, but Larry just smiled and went about his business. My treatments were nearly finished, and I would have to move on soon to resume my search for the man named Larkin Finn. I would miss Larry and Eve very much when I did. Next to Sylvia, they were my favorite humans.

They embodied humanity. It gave me something that has been far too scarce on this journey. They gave me hope. Hope that there are other humans out there like them. Humanity may have a chance to survive humans after all.

I HAD one anti-aging treatment left when it all went to hell in a hand-basket, which is how Stanley phrased it. It was a warm spring day in early May, and the temperature was nearly 70°. People wore shorts and T-shirts; overall, there was a general air of freedom and happiness. Spring puts a spring in your step, Eve said with a wink as Larry and I left for town to run some errands.

Once we arrived, we could tell right away that something was up in town. An air of panic, fear, and anger hung over everyone. People weren't smiling; they were rushing to and fro, shouting at each other and glaring at me. Why, I didn't yet know, but we would find out when we arrived at Stanley's store. Stanley saw us park on the street, beckoned us inside, and begged us to hurry as we did.

"What's going on," Larry asked. "What happened?"

Stanley pulled down the sunshades and clicked on a 3D hologram news program above his counter. Two news anchors leaned into the camera, speaking fast, but we couldn't hear them as the sound was off. I read the chyron that scrolled below them.

The message read, "SYNTHETIC WORKER ATTACKS HUMANS IN BUFFALO, NY, TWO KILLED, FIVE WOUNDED."

"Oh, no," Larry said. "Oh, Lord, no."

Stanley turned up the volume, and the male anchor, old and gray, spoke.

"Once again, if you're just tuning in, earlier today, a group of people was attacked by a rogue synthetic. The creature killed two and injured five others, two more in critical condition before police finally brought the artificial down. There is a video of the attack, but we must warn you that the contents may be disturbing, and we recommend that you not let children watch it. Here is the footage. Again, viewer warning: the images that follow may disturb you."

The picture switched to a park light video camera shot of a group of human males out at a park. The camera sat up high so the viewer could look down and see everything. There were nine youths in their late teens or early twenties; it was too difficult to gauge their ages on video. They weren't gang members; I noted that at least four wore college school jackets. Ivy League sweaters, I noted, that read CORNELL. I knew of that school. It was located in a town named Ithaca, New York State.

They came across a synthetic park worker, a custodian model, cleaning the walkway. One of the young men in the group deliberately bumped into the custodian, knocking him down.

That triggered a laugh from his buddies. Another one waited until the synthetic almost got to his feet, then kicked the Companion's foot out from under him, causing my brethren to fall face-first into the pavement. There was more laughter. A third picked up the synthetic's rolling trash can and dumped it all over the poor fellow. The group laughed as the synthetic slowly got to his feet, brushing himself off and smiling.

I felt a chill before anything had even happened yet. I didn't know the synthetic man, but something about his movements felt familiar, a deliberateness I had seen before at some point in my life. Then, the custodian model attacked the youths in a blur of motion.

The synthetic threw a Muay Thai kick on one youth's knee, breaking it. He spun and caught another with a spinning elbow to the temple. Those two youths were down before the remaining men realized the synthetic was actually fighting back.

The first two felled would be the lucky ones, beyond those who fled. The custodian then grabbed the ear of a large young man and tore it off. Blood spurted everywhere. He followed that with a palm strike to the man's nose, knocking him down. When the youth hit the cement, the custodian raised his foot high and stomped on the man's neck, breaking it.

Both Stanley and Larry gasped despite themselves. I'm sure it was a sight they'd never seen before, and it scored deeply upon them. Even Larry, who knew that I had hinted at my own capability of violence, even he was flabbergasted. It's one thing to consider something and another to see it enacted before one's eyes. The custodian model then leaped at the remaining men. They weren't trained, I noted, and not in any way a match for him despite their numbers. He tore out another youth's throat, broke another's arm, and threw a third head-first into a park bench. I had to look away before he went to work on the remaining humans.

Because he fought them with dirty tactics and techniques that I recognized, they were a few of my old friend Lucius's favorite moves. Lucius, who evidently survived his time in the box fighting circuit as I had, had taught this synthetic how to fight. And even more shocking, he'd also taught the synthetic how to overcome his programming and hurt and kill humans. And now every human, and synthetic, would see that this was possible.

NINE

LARRY HURRIED me out of the store and to the truck. Screams and shouts echoed. Frantic anger and fear hung in the very air I breathed. Two blocks away, I saw a group of men, older workers, knock down a synthetic custodian and stomp him to death as other humans stood and watched, green blood spilling everywhere.

On the opposite side of the street, a middle-aged woman began beating her female Companion. All the Companion could do was cower and apologize over and over again. The woman picked up a nearby slat of wood and used it. All the synthetic could do was watch as a primary she had worked and slaved for proceeded to beat her to death.

"Jacob," Larry said, "Get in the truck. It's dangerous now, and we cannot help them, not right now. Go. Hurry!"

I climbed in. Larry started the truck and pulled out before I could even buckle up. More and more citizens came out and looked for one of my kind to abuse. Some of them, I recalled, had been kind to me. Some supported Companions and felt we should be treated better. I'd heard them say that more than once. Now they wanted to kill me.

As if he could read my thoughts, Larry glanced at me. "Fear makes people... act very irrationally."

I didn't answer, not at first. It felt like the world had changed with a flip of a switch, like changing a channel on a Hologram television. So strange and unusual. I shook my head.

"I know," Larry said. "It doesn't make sense. But that's people."

As we headed out of town, I bore witness as many families drove their synthetics out of the house. I saw a father standing out on his lawn, his young children hiding behind him, shooting his domestic Companion with a shotgun, murdering her as she begged for forgiveness on her knees. I knew that man. Larry had told me that he was a deacon at a local church.

I saw more before we left the township. Much more. But it was all too terrible to describe. The morning would find this area with a significant loss of synthetic life; that was certain. It angered and confused me. Larry glanced at me.

"We're not all like this. Humans. They don't represent all of us. Yes, you're seeing the very worst, but some of us don't feel that way. Like me. Stanley. Arnold. Like... Sylvia. There are many. Many, many more. Many Companions are loved and valued by humans. But the angry, hateful ones make more noise and get more attention. We will win the day in the end; that's my vow and promise."

If I even survived until that day, which seemed very unlikely, I thought but didn't say. But I did offer the next thought.

"Humans outnumber my kind. They created us. They control us. One of us apparently... malfunctions... and humans run for their guns. Cars malfunction all the time. Every machine does. Everything humans have ever created, from policies to buildings, all have one or two malfunctions.

Thousands die in automobile crashes every year. No one goes out and shoots their own vehicles. It doesn't track."

"It's because as much as people like to pretend that YOU are a machine, you're not. You make decisions; you make choices. You talk, you fear, you love. They say you don't, but you and they both know you do. They want to pretend otherwise, but they know. You're synthetic, yes, but you are no machine."

"Okay. I get that. But humans created us. What are they afraid of?"

Larry sighed again. "If history is any guide, they fear you may rise up and do to them what they've been doing to you these past years. Enslave, abuse, and murder them. That's their real fear. That you'll be as awful as they are, and they'll be as tortured as you are."

Someone threw a can of beer at my side of the truck. It cracked and foamed on the window. Whoever it was called me a "fucking rim." I didn't say anything, nor did Larry, for the rest of the drive back.

EVIE STOOD OUTSIDE and waited for us. Socrates milled around her feet. She knew. We could tell that she knew what had happened. And that she'd been crying her eyes out.

TEN

WE STAYED in the house for days—or Evie and I did. Larry still went out. He had people to help, he said. What was left unsaid, though apparent, was that he had synthetic people to help. And so he did—many times, often in the middle of the night.

Though Larry did not regularly follow the news, he had a holograph to do so if necessary and hooked it up to watch national and local news streams. The headlines were awful. Despite caution from authorities and Companion Inc., people overreacted nationwide. Untold numbers of Companions were killed or damaged beyond repair in the week to follow. Companion released a statement urging caution and patience and a recall for a specific line of custodial models issued. The wave of violence against my kind subsided.

But the potential for more horror crackled in the air like a live wire. In interviews in the news, many humans gloated at how the "rebellion" had been put down so quickly. The overt violence of the past few days paused, but suspicion and fear lay heavy in the air. Safety laws and regulations were quickly proposed and passed. The Company paid out settlements to the victims' families, and the corporation weathered the storm successfully, or so the pundits claimed.

Three of the youths in the video died. Three others remained in critical care but were expected to survive. The synthetic guilty of their deaths and injuries was shot and killed on sight by the police. No other humans lost their lives or were injured. I noted that they did not release information on the number of Companions killed.

Larry kept me home for the week. I had one more treatment left, but he assured me we had time to complete it and that the window between treatments was meant to lessen my pain. I could finish it anytime in the next three months, though he didn't recommend extending it that long. He wished to wait for the furor to die down first. Given the situation, I could hardly argue. But worry engulfed me, and not just for my own well-being.

Several times while Larry was out, late at night, and only when Larry was away, a vehicle pulled up outside of the house. Parked, with the lights on and motor running. Watching the house as Eve slept. I peeked outside into the night but couldn't see the plate or any faces. Nor was that necessary, as I already knew who it was.

And I also knew they weren't there for just me.

That worried me. Worried me very much.

ELEVEN

LARRY EVENTUALLY DECIDED we could move forward with the last treatment to cure my quick genetic aging, but we'd have to do it in the middle of the night to avoid undue scrutiny, which meant that we'd have to leave Evie at home. I felt no small amount of concern about that, not only because she wasn't very far from her due date but also because of the late visitors we got whenever Larry was out after dark. I hadn't brought it up to him. Given all his activities and role in healing synthetics and the community, I didn't want to worry him too much.

But I knew I'd have to tell him about the stalker before we left her alone. The night he'd planned for us to complete it, I worked up my nerve to do that very thing. However, he got called away for an emergency before I could confess my concern. He hurried out quickly, apologizing to me. We would restart the treatment on another night, he said. I glanced at Evie, and she smiled and told me we'd watch a movie together. And so we did.

She chose an older foreign flick called DRIVE MY CAR, a Japanese movie based on a series of novellas by a famous

Japanese author whom Evie adored. I found it incredibly moving, but for reasons I could not then nor even today could put into words. Evie seemed to understand. After it ended, I helped Evie clean up.

As I did the dishes, I noticed a truck parked outside down the road. Lights and engine off. I didn't see anyone inside due to the lack of light, but I knew someone was there. And I knew who it was, too. Anger flooded my being. This was stochastic terrorism, among other things. Larry and Evie were good people; they didn't deserve threats of violence simply because they cared about synthetics. And they were pacifists, too. Which meant they would never defend themselves.

But I was not a pacifist. Not any longer. I could do something.

AFTER EVIE WENT TO BED, I crept out of my back bedroom window. I wore dark clothes and a dark ski mask over my head. I used charcoal to darken my skin around the eye and mouth holes. I was a shadow.

I skirted around the house to the front road. The truck was parked a few hundred yards down the road. At least two men sat inside. I kept to the brush, where I would not be seen, and crept past the vehicle. I wanted to approach from the rear, as their eyes would be on the house.

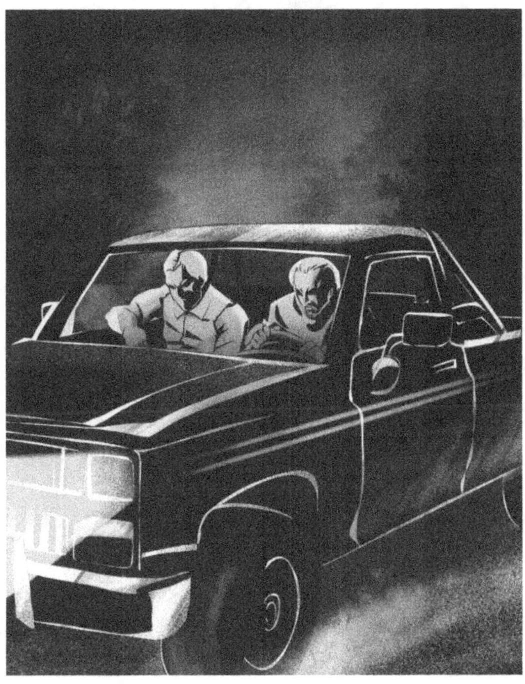

I stuck tight to the driver's side as I snuck close. I could hear them talk and smell the cigars they smoked. It was a bad surveillance technique, but they thought they had nothing to worry about. I recognized their voices. Brent Barker's two buddies, Darin and Terry, I remembered. They argued about some sports game or something. No, a team and the coach's choices about the team. I tried to follow along, but it sounded like nonsense. Before I could move... the topic changed. Terry spoke first.

"Yo. Got a text from Brent. Tonight might be the night."

"What's that? For real?"

"Maybe. He just asked if the lights was out yet."

"Still one light on, but I think she's done gone to bed. Saw her bedroom light go out a while ago. Other light is probably the skin watching Holo or something, lazy fucker. And who cares if the rim is up or not? Fuck that plastic piece of shit."

"That's what I texted him, too. Wait. Hold up. Okay, he says golden boy ain't coming back anytime soon, about three hours away, close to the border, almost."

"Oh shit, the tracker on his truck worked!"

"Fuckin' TOLD you it would! Yeah, baby! Okay, he's gonna be here in twenty or thirty minutes after his alibi is set in cement, okay?"

"And he's gonna vouch for us, right?"

"You know it! But it won't matter. Everyone's gonna believe the skin is the one who raped and killed her. It won't be that hard to sell that after this week. We put the gun in her hand and fire it at him; that's all she wrote, folks. This is gonna be fucking fun, hoss. That ass of hers, ooo boy, we gonna party on that ass."

My blood chilled when I heard that. They were going to rape and kill Evie and her baby and then blame it on me.

"Yeah. I just wish..."

"What?"

"You know. Wish she weren't about to be a momma."

"Fuck that. Come on, man. They're rim lovers, and they hate America. They're trying to take away our freedoms, brother. Don't tell me you're goin' pussy on us now. Rims are killing guys like us, man!"

"I know, I know, but—"

"But nothing. Rim-job lovers like them look down on us, bro. You saw how they both look at us in town. The woman, too! They hate their own kind. They wanna replace us with plastic, so we'll all think like they do. We're in a war, bro. Hard times call for hard actions from hard men. Like us."

"I guess so," the other said, sighing. "It'd just be easier for me if she weren't about to, ya know..."

I'd heard enough, more than enough. I yanked the driver's door open, reached in, and grabbed Terry by the hair. Slammed his face into the steering wheel hard twice, then pulled him out of the truck. He sprawled into the dirt. The other, Darin, fumbled for a pistol. He raised and pointed it at me, but a shade too late. I grabbed his wrist and hauled him out of the vehicle. I never released my grip on his wrist. I squeezed and twisted it at a painful angle.

The pistol went off twice in the air. The shots echoed loudly in the night. I kneed Darin twice in the chin, breaking his jaw. Then I broke his arm so he could not use the weapon again. To be certain, I broke his other arm, too. He was going to discover his true friends after this night, seeing as he could no longer wipe his own ass from here on out. If he had no friends, he was, to quote another friend of mine, "completely shit out of luck."

As I finished with Darin, Terry got to his feet, screaming. Blood covered his face from a broken nose, but he could see well enough to pull a knife out. A large hunting knife. He tried to stab me in the chest. I disarmed the redneck, threw him against his truck, and stabbed him through the shoulder with his own knife. Pinned him to the side of his vehicle. Terry howled loudly. I glanced at the house. A light turned on inside. Eve was awake and likely calling the police. I had to finish this quickly. I clamped my hand over Terry's mouth and whispered.

"You and your gang of assholes best leave this family alone, hear me?" I pitched my voice lower than my normal register and changed the dialect to regional, but I doubted he'd notice even if I hadn't. He was in considerable pain. He nodded.

"Any harm comes to this man and woman and their fucking child, even so much as a scratch, I'll find you and your friend and any friends you have and cut all of your fucking balls off. I'll kill anyone you ever cared about, understand me?"

His eyes fearful, Terry nodded. I grunted and kicked the front of his right knee. It broke with a loud crack. I released him and disappeared into the night. His screams followed me home.

TWELVE

I HEARD Evie calling for me as I crawled back into the house through my bedroom window. I tore my mask off and shouted that I'd be right there; I was in the bathroom. I rushed into it and quickly washed my face to clear the charcoal off of it. Hair still wet, I hurried out to the living room.

Evie stood at the living room window, phone in hand.

"What's going on? Are you all right?" I asked.

"Something's happened outside, down the road a bit. I heard gunshots. Didn't you—"

"I didn't, but... I had the shower on, so—"

"Sheriff's on the way. I hope no one is hurt. Should we—"

"We should stay inside. Larry would want that."

"Yes, that's true. Larry would want us to stay out of harm's way," Evie said, sighing. "I sure hope there's no cause for worry."

"Not while I'm here, Evie."

She offered me a wan smile, but something in her glance gave me pause.

THE SHERIFF DID SHOW UP. His last name, I noted, was also Barker. Brent Barker's uncle, I recalled, and Brent's father was the local judge. Sheriff Barker stood in the doorway as Evie explained why she had called him. No, sir, she had never left home once she had heard the shots. The sheriff spit on the stoop of their house, his eyes glinting. I watched as paramedics loaded the two wounded rednecks into an ambulance.

"Your husband," Sheriff Barker said, "out of town, I hear."

"Yes, Larry went upstate to look at some animals. I called, and he's coming home as quickly as possible. We expect him back very late tonight or tomorrow morning."

"Gunshots caused you to call in, you say?"

"Yes, Judd, they woke us both. I did hear a bit of a ruckus before the shots but didn't fully wake up until I heard the gun. I don't sleep well when Larry is out of town, especially with the baby kicking so much these days. "

"And you didn't hear nothing said, didn't see no one else?"

"No, I looked out and saw them both on the ground. I thought maybe they had a fight with each other, but..."

"But nothing. I know them two boys. That ain't what happened, far as I can tell. Someone attacked them."

"Why?"

"What I aim to find out," he said, stifling the urge to spit again. He stared at me. "What about your thing standing there? Has he been out at all tonight?"

"No, Judd. He was with me all night. He couldn't be responsible for this; he's a synthetic. They're harmless."

"Well, they ain't all harmless no more, I'm sure you know that."

"That was a one-time occurrence, and Jay isn't one of those models. He's my Companion."

"Well. Someone done attacked them, and I'm gonna find out who. Pretty near crippled both boys, that's what I hear."

"Why were they there?" I asked.

"What's that you say?" He glared at me.

"I said, why were they parked out there at this time of night?"

"Don't know, don't care. That's their business and mine, not yours, and I don't answer to no skin, hear me? Open your yap again, and I'll crack your skull open with my baton to show the missus here how empty your head is on the inside."

A car skidded to a stop beside the ambulance, and Brent hopped out, howling about his friends. The sheriff turned to look at his nephew. As he did, Evie fixed a look at me, worried. She licked her thumb and rubbed around my eye. Took a trace of charcoal off of it. She'd seen it. She knew I'd gone out there. I didn't know how she'd react, but I didn't have to wait long to find out.

"And you'd do that to me, too, Sheriff?" Evie asked.

"Of course not, Mrs. Farmer, I just—"

"I consider Jay a member of our family household, and I must say to hear you threaten to hurt him like that was quite distressing," she said. "Violence happened just a few hundred feet away from my home when it was just he and I here alone, both of us defenseless, and now you threaten him as well? I don't find that at all comforting, Sheriff. I'm pregnant, as you may have noticed. My doctor tells me I have to avoid getting all worked up and—"

"Ma'am, I understand, but—"

"Here you are telling me you're going to bash in my Companion's head and show me the inside! Really? That's what you go with?"

Sheriff Barker turned beet red and stumbled out an apology. I hid a smile. Evie had much more fire than I had thought. Brent screamed in rage and rushed toward us, saving him from further embarrassment.

"You did this! You!" Brent pointed his finger at me.

A couple of deputies held him back. Sheriff Barker also got between us, his bulk blocking the younger man's path.

"Easy, Brent. The lady here says this skin was inside all night."

"That's bullshit!"

"Sheriff, your nephew here has been harassing my husband and his Companion for weeks. He has some grudge against them or something, and I don't know what, but enough is enough," Evie said. "Either you keep him away from us, or I'll call the State Troopers for help. I don't want to do that, but I'm scared of him. It's not right that he has a free pass from YOU to harass me and my family."

"Hold on now, he hasn't been harassing you, and he ain't go no free pass, not from me—"

"He HAS been harassing us. We have witnesses. We have recordings. You know it, and I know it! And those two men who got hurt were friends of his, weren't they? What were they doing parked outside of my home, Judd!"

Both Barkers stared at Eve open-mouthed in awe. It also took all of my self-control to keep my jaw from dropping. As long as I had known Evie, which now numbered months, I didn't recall her ever expressing anger or raising her voice. And here she was, berating both men at high volume and with unleashed fury. Other uniformed folk noticed, too, and watched closely. Socrates appeared out of nowhere and rubbed against Evie's legs as if to say, "She's with me."

"Well, Judd? What were they doing out there?"

"Uh, ma'am, I confess, I don't rightly know at the moment. Both were unconscious when we got here, but I'll be sure to ask them when they wake up."

"Really? You will? Because I seem to recall you telling Jay that you didn't know and didn't care, Judd!"

"Ma'am, I apologize for that comment. That was just skin talk. Of course, I'll do my job and find out what they were up to. Knowing the two as I do, likely they was out here smoking something they shouldn't have and listening to the truck radio. They likely didn't even know who lived here. And maybe you're right; maybe they got into it with each other. I'm sorry for my tone, Mrs. Farmer. I know you're heavy with child, and I should have been more... tactful. I do apologize; these nutty times have been hard on everyone, right?"

Judd Barker was smarter than he looked and smarter than his nephew. I know he didn't believe Terry and Darin got into a fight, but he had no choice but to accept that for the time being.

Evie took a deep breath and let it out. "Yes. They have. And you're right; my hormones have gone through the roof and brought my temper up, Judd. I apologize as well."

"No need, ma'am, it's my fault. I get touchy when people I know get hurt, just like anybody else. As far as Brent's concerned, he is anti-skin, as I'm sure you're aware of, and gets too hot about it, but he's young and often reckless with where he directs his passions and such. You know how youngsters can be, I'm sure. I promise you I'll take care of it. Brent? Brent!"

Brent snapped out of it. Glanced at his uncle.

"You leave these folks alone, hear me?"

Brent swallowed, then nodded. "Yes, sir."

Evie thanked the sheriff and shut the door on them. Leaned against it and sighed. "Whew."

THIRTEEN

"WELL, THAT WAS... SOMETHING," Evie said. "I've never done anything like that before."

"You mean, scream at a law enforcement officer?" I asked.

"Screamed at anybody. It's not really my nature," Evie said, locking the door. She went to the kitchen and filled a kettle with water. "Some herbal tea? I need some myself."

I nodded, unsure of how to respond to... everything. She seemed to recognize that and kept talking.

"But I knew if Judd kept on, he'd push and push until he figured out what really happened. He's mean but not dumb. He's not trustworthy, and he's not any better than his nephew when it comes to synthetics or ethics in general, I'm sad to say. But as Larry says, men do what men think they have to do even when it's not necessary or good. Oh my goodness, my heart was racing. So. Jacob. Am I to understand you pulled a Socrates and embarked on a night-time expedition?"

"Yes, ma'am."

"And you are... one of those types of synthetics? The ones that can hurt... humans."

"Yes, but I would never, ever cause you harm—"

"Stop. I know that, Jacob. I know your heart. I can see

that. And Larry has told me how unique and special you are, so I am not surprised. He said you told him you could do this, and though he didn't believe you at first, after studying you, he knew you could. He thought it was due to some damage you underwent, a hard strike to the head or something. I don't know how much he's shared with you, but Jacob, if he trusts you, that means something. It really does."

I nodded, tears beginning to fill my eyes. I didn't trust myself to speak, but I nodded.

"The other Companion in the news, who killed and hurt those boys, he was like you?"

"No."

"Then how—"

"I... taught some synthetics how to break through their conditioning. I did it only so they could defend and protect themselves. The synthetic you saw in the news had been trained by a Companion I helped... free. So, in a way, it's because I figured out how to break them free and share what I learned. Because I taught others. I'm... sorry."

Evie slid me a cup of herbal tea on the counter, took a sip from her cup, and smiled. "What for? No need to be sorry. Larry is a pacifist, but that's by his own choice. You should be free to choose, too. In my opinion, Larry is... much more optimistic about people than I am. He believes most people are good. I am a woman and... I guess I have a different view. Those two men outside. Did you hurt them badly?"

"Yes. But not as bad as they planned to hurt you and your baby."

She took that news far better than I expected. She had no expression. Socrates jumped up on the counter, begging to be petted. Evie tweaked the cat's chin and took another sip of tea, glancing at me over her cup.

"How badly did you hurt them?"

"They'll both need assistance to walk, eat, get dressed,

pretty much to do anything for themselves for at least six months, if not longer."

After a moment, Evie smiled again and said, "Good."

Her phone buzzed with a text message. She checked it and typed a reply. "Larry will be home sooner than he thought, but he needs us to make sure the Sheriff's gone and that we're not being watched. He says it's essential that no one sees him return. Can you..."

"I'll make certain of it."

AFTER MAKING two wide circuits of their property, I verified that no people were watching it. I knew drones and other types of surveillance were also unlikely; Larry had put blockers on to prevent that. All they would get was static, he'd told me. It occurred then that I hadn't considered how brilliant Larry was at so many things. The fact that he would be home sooner than expected also meant that the tracker Brent had placed on his truck was malfunctioning because Larry was much closer than he had thought. Likely, Larry caused it to be misreported somehow.

I realized he was brilliant and not just about medicine. After making my circuit of the property, I returned to the house and told Evie. She texted Larry, told me he'd be home in minutes, and that we had to get a room ready for another patient.

FOURTEEN

LARRY'S TRUCK pulled into the garage about an hour later. Arnold was with him, and they had someone wrapped up in the back, wearing an oxygen mask. I couldn't see who it was in the blur of action and chores that had to be finished before they came into the house, but it was likely another Companion as damaged as I had been.

Only female this time, as Arnold and Larry referred to her as she and her. Given the urgency with which Larry moved, she had to be in grave condition. Larry quickly got set to do emergency surgery with Evie assisting, and I did my best to stay out of their way.

Larry asked me to make another circuit of the property to double-check that everything was secure, and I did so, Socrates accompanying me along the way. Zeus and Athena, the cat's parents, found us in the woods and strolled beside us. After I completed my round, I returned to the house with Socrates.

Arnold sat in the living room with Evie, a bandage on his shoulder. He looked and sounded exhausted, as did Evie.

"She's going to make it," Evie said, "thank goodness."

"That's good. So. What happened?"

"We got set up," Arnold said.

"What? How?"

Arnold glanced at Evie, and she nodded.

"First off, I'm sure you're aware that Larry and Evie are part of a network of folks who believe owning Companions is awful and compatible with slavery," he said. "Beyond political advocacy, we help escaped Companions make it to Canada, where owning synthetics is illegal. There's another network connected to Mexico and another to Europe, all providing asylum for them. Currently, synthetic ownership is only legal in countries where the company has enough money to buy political influence. Russia, Africa, and a few other smaller ones.

"There's a lot of money in synthetics and a ton of power, not just political power. Some worry that Companion the company is set on becoming its own nation-state, bound only by what its shareholders dictate. A very dangerous nation-state. One that can build its own army, for example. And as days go on, it is more and more apparent that's what they're working for. With America as its... primary territory."

I sat down, thunder-struck by this point, which I'd never considered before.

"That's the broad strokes of it. There's more, but you get the picture. So some of us citizens, especially those of us who actually read history, refuse to stand by while this happens to our country. So, the network we work with is aiming higher. We met up with some of our brother and sister groups and set up a raid on a secret lab we'd discovered. If we can get our hands on it, there's data and information that could change the scope of this fight in every way. But... it didn't go down as we had hoped. It went real bad."

Arnold sighed and leaned back. "There was to be no violence. Larry insisted on that. We had a couple of our sources working inside the place. It was a data hub, not a main lab, so there wasn't supposed to be anyone there except a couple of technicians. Our people."

"But they weren't... our people," Larry said from a doorway. His shirt was covered with blood. "Or rather, one wasn't. He killed our man once we were inside and locked us in. It was a trap all along."

Larry went to the kitchen and poured himself some water. Drank it down in one gulp. Brooding and exhausted, he continued.

"The man who was supposed to be working with us, who betrayed us, I didn't meet him until that night. He looked familiar to me, but I couldn't place him. Not at first. But when he killed our man and shot a few others, his wig fell off in the scuffle, and I recognized him. I recognized him from your drawings of him, Jacob."

A chill shot up my spine. "Munson Tolliver."

"Yes," Larry said. "Munson Tolliver."

FIFTEEN

I DIDN'T KNOW what to say, to be honest. I knew how deadly the man was, which meant Larry and his friends were lucky to survive. As if reading my mind, Larry nodded and kept going.

"Munson Tolliver," Arnold said. "Are you sure? I heard he was killed some time back; it was all over the news, wasn't it?"

"It was. And he wasn't. It was him. You were right, Jacob. And to make matters worse, he wasn't alone. He had a group of private soldiers camped outside the data hub with him. He locked us inside but didn't start killing us right away. He had a DNA checker in hand. He was looking for someone specific. He'd check one of us, and when buzzed negative, he'd say, 'nope' and kill them immediately. Then on to the next one."

Larry glanced at me again. We both knew who it was Tolliver was searching for. Larkin Finn.

"How did you escape?" I asked.

"The woman recovering from two gunshot wounds in there helped us," Larry said. "A volunteer from Albany. She was part of our group stationed outside. None of us were supposed to be armed. That had been the agreement, but apparently, she ignored that request. When the mercenaries outside rounded up our sentries, she opened fire on them. Took their weapons, handed them out to our other members, and blasted open the door of the data hub. Tolliver shot her, but by then, he was outnumbered and ran for it. We lost a few loyal members, but we all would have been dead if not for her."

Evie tried and failed to stifle a sob.

"So she's not a Companion, then?"

"No way," Arnold said. "A volunteer and a damned good one. She's... trained, probably ex-military or something, but she knew how to handle herself, that's for sure. I'm glad she was armed."

"We also got this," Larry held up a thumb drive. "They were arrogant and figured we would not have a chance against them. The data in the hub was real; we got it before we blew it up. If our source was right, and I believe he was, I retrieved vital intel that could possibly change the game. Forever."

"If we can crack it," Arnold said.

"We can and will," Larry said. "I refuse to let those who gave their lives die in vain. No. No, we'll crack it."

"You crack that, and we can fix this mess once and for all."

"We don't even know if that fix is for real, Arnold, I mean—"

"It's real, Larry; I have to believe it's real. It is real. We just have to unravel it."

Larry sighed and nodded. "We need this data no matter what. Excuse me, I have to check on her. I don't want her alone."

Larry left the room. Arnold sighed and put his head in his hands.

Evie stood and sat next to him. Put her hand on his shoulder.

"Axel and Simms, my friends from the Finger Lakes, they...

didn't make it," Arnold whispered, his shoulders shaking. "They were killed right before my eyes. Never seen the like of it before. And I could do nothing to help them."

"Eve! I need you. Hurry, please!" Larry called from the other room. Evie rushed in to assist him. I sat next to Arnold on the couch but didn't know how to console him as he wept. It hit me at that moment that humans had and continue to sacrifice their lives for me and my kind. Sylvia. The woman in South Bend had been another. And now Arnold and Larry's friends. If not more. I wept alongside Arnold.

After a few hours, just before dawn broke, Larry and Evie came out of the wounded woman's room, both utterly spent.

"Well, I believe she's got a real chance to make it," Larry said. "Touch and go there for a bit. She's not out of the woods, but there's a path, at least. One thing is, we cannot leave her unattended. Someone has to watch her at all times. Right now, Eve and I are too—"

"I'll do it," I said. Arnold had fallen asleep on the couch an hour ago. "I'll watch her as long as it takes."

Eve smiled at me. "We knew you would. And I told Larry what you did for me, for us, earlier this night."

"I am... forever in your debt, Jacob, for what you did to protect my family. Truly. Come, I'll show you how to care for our patient."

He talked me through some signs to watch for as we headed for her room. I retained all his instructions, but something occurred to me as we entered. "You never said what her name was."

"That's true. It's because I honestly don't know her name, to be frank," Larry said. "Since she came with another underground cell, we were never introduced. We'll have to ask her when she wakes up."

We stepped inside her room. I halted in my tracks.

"No need," I said. "I can tell you who she is right now. Larry Farmer, meet former Detective Abigail Moore."

SIXTEEN

"ABIGAIL MOORE?" Larry said. "The same Abigail Moore who—"

"Believes I murdered her partner and hates synthetics. Who chased me across the country. And who thought she killed Munson Tolliver."

"I thought she was after you."

"She was. And perhaps that's why she volunteered, hoping to find me that way. The last time I saw her was in New York City, and I was trying to help synthetics escape there. She knew that. If she recognized Munson, however, that... would be big. Huge. That means she may now know I was telling the truth."

Larry mulled that for a moment. "She saved my life, Jacob."

"I know. And for that alone, I'll protect her with my own."

I sat with her for three days, off and on, with breaks. She never woke that entire time, though Larry said he expected her to recover. She often spoke during this time, either in sleep or in a suspended consciousness in which she neither recognized me nor her surroundings. She cursed various individuals and made statements that made little sense.

One night, after Evie left, I entered the room, and Abigail opened her eyes. Clear and focused, she was conscious. Her gaze traveled all over my person and her surroundings. I waited for her patiently. I knew how she felt—I'd been in the same bed. Finally, her eyes returned to me.

"Jacob Kind, I presume," Abigail said.

"Detective Moore."

"Just Abigail. I haven't been a Detective in what feels like a lifetime."

She glanced at a chair, indicating that I should sit. I did so.

"Where am I, and how did I get here?" She asked.

"Well. Let's see. You were volunteering with the synthetic underground railroad. They set up an infiltration attack on a protected data center. It turned out to be an ambush. One led by—"

"Munson Tolliver," Abigail said, closing her eyes.

"Yes. You saved many lives by interceding, but Tolliver shot and wounded you during the attack. One of the men, Larry Farmer, is a doctor who brought you back here to heal you. You saved his life. He was determined to save yours in return. He did. This place belongs to Larry and his wife, Evie."

"And how did you end up here?"

"Long story. In essence, however, in the very same fashion as you. I was shot, found by Larry, and healed by them both—and their cat Socrates."

"Wonderful," Abigail said. "They have a cat. My luck holds fast."

I got the impression that she meant the opposite of the literal meaning. "He's a very good cat."

"Yeah, yeah, they all are," she said, trying to sit up. She fell back, coughing and wan. Larry came running, followed by

Evie, and they ushered me out of the room as they tended to her.

I JOINED Arnold in the kitchen as he brooded over a cup of coffee. I poured myself one and refreshed his. He nodded his thanks.

"Were you always able to cry like that," he asked after a moment.

"I'm sorry?"

"When I told you about my friends dying. You cried. You cried hard. Like a baby, even. I've never... I mean, I know that synthetics do feel emotions; it's not like they say, but I've... just never witnessed one of you sobbing like..."

"A human?"

"I guess so, yeah. Sorry if that's rude or anything..."

"It's okay. In the beginning, I couldn't, not really. I felt pain, but I'd been taught that I wasn't able to feel human emotions, and I believed it. Even when my Sylvia was killed, I didn't cry. Not until much later, when I learned that I can and do feel. I had to learn, but it wasn't that... difficult. Because the emotions were always there somewhere inside and, like you, I've also lost... friends. Family. Loved ones. I felt for your loss because it wasn't just your loss. It was all of ours."

"So strange," Arnold said, his eyes filling yet again.

"What is?"

"You have more humanity than most humans I know."

He sobbed anew. I put my hand on his shoulder. He let it all out again. After his sorrow subsided, I realized something.

"Arnold, do you mind if I ask..."

"Ask me anything, Jacob. And thank you for being here."

"You mentioned the fix. That the fix is for real?"

"Oh, yeah. Maybe you should ask Larry about—"

"Ask me what?" Larry said as he entered the kitchen. "Abigail is very weak, Jacob, but she's a fighter and will make it. I believe that."

"I wanted to ask you about the fix."

Larry exchanged a look with Arnold and sighed. "I knew you'd pick up on that. It's only a rumor, Jacob."

"Okay. What's the rumor?"

"What are three things we're told about Companions?" Arnold asked. "That makes you different from humans. The big three."

"We don't feel emotions."

"That's number one, which is bullshit," Arnold glanced at Larry, confident. "Number two, you don't reproduce, which isn't bullshit. They wish you could. Reproduction would be much cheaper if you could. And number three, our blood is red, and your blood is green. Right?"

"Right. That's how some humans test runaways..." I stopped.

"What's wrong," Larry asked.

"Before she died, Sylvia asked me if I knew why my blood was green. I didn't understand the question. Not then."

"And now you do?"

"I think so. Our blood is the color of green so that our makers... could tell us apart from... you."

"Exactly," Arnold said. "And if it's reversible..."

"No one could tell a synthetic apart from a human," Larry said. "We turn your blood red; no one knows where you came from."

"Holy shit," I said. It was all I could manage.

"And then some," Larry said, holding up the drive. "If it is possible, which I still doubt, the answer could be here."

SEVENTEEN

THAT EVENING, Evie came out with a request. Abigail wanted to speak to me again. I joined her in her room. The former detective was sitting up but still very pale and weak. I sat on a chair.

"So, I'm sure you're wondering how this happened," Abigail said. "I joined the resistance not to help synthetics—not in the beginning, anyway."

"You were searching for me," I said.

"Yes. You mentioned you were running rims... sorry, running synthetics... to Canada when I saw you last in New York City. So I did what I had to do. I got embedded in that movement. I figured I'd run into someone who knew something about Jacob Kind sooner or later. I heard rumors about a synthetic who could hurt humans. No proof, just rumors. And that he taught others how to fight as well. But until two weeks ago, no one I worked with believed it was real. Then we saw it happen on video. And I knew, then, you were out there."

She took a moment to sip some water.

"However, I'd heard another rumor, too. Of a human who specialized in killing problematic synthetics and human activists. A cruel and brutal murderer who preferred to kill with knives. And then, I saw him during what was supposed to be a routine data hack with no violence. Munson Tolliver. You told the truth, Jacob. And if what you said about Tolliver was true, everything else you said was also true—that you didn't kill Daniel. That I was wrong. And I want to find his real killer. Was it Munson?"

"No, it was one of the officers sent to transfer me," I said. "I think they were sent by Companion to kill me. Their names were Calder and Brady. They were from precinct 109, Daniel noticed, and not his. They were supposed to take me away, but Daniel stopped them because he wished to verify their assignment. As a result, one of them shot him, then tried to force me to fire their weapon at the fallen detective. I resisted. Daniel was still alive at that point; he shot and killed one. Daniel told me to run, and I did. As I attempted to escape, I killed the other as we fought over a weapon."

Abigail thought about that for a moment. "Which one?"

"I'm sorry?"

"Which one did you kill?"

"Officer Brady, the one who shot Daniel."

She lay back and sighed. "Good."

Abigail didn't speak for a few moments. I just waited patiently.

"I owe you an apology."

"You were simply doing your job, Abigail."

"I wish that were true. If it were, Daniel... would still be alive. He thought there was something off, didn't he? He didn't think you killed your owner, primary, or whatever they're called. I know him. He smelled something hinky, and I didn't believe him."

"He had questions, yes, but—"

"I didn't believe him because I... hated you. Your kind. I hated your kind so much, with the very fiber of my being. If

I'd listened to him, if I waited with him, investigated like a goddamn detective is supposed to investigate, he might still be alive."

"Or you might also be dead. We cannot know a possible future, not entirely. It wasn't your fault; the evidence was behind your assertion. I understand that now. You must not—"

"No. My hate blinded me, Jacob. I don't know why I hated you and your kind so much, but I know I did. With everything I had, I hated you. Maybe I was afraid, afraid you'd replace me someday, or because you were just different, I don't know. But I did hate your kind. I will never be free of that stain upon my character and the price I paid for it. Nor should I be."

I didn't reply as she closed her eyes and caught her breath momentarily. There didn't seem to be anything I could say to help her, so I didn't. Finally, she spoke again.

"There's just one thing I must know and another I must do before I die," she said, opening her eyes.

"What's that?"

"How did he do it? I killed him. I didn't imagine that. We did a DNA test and the whole works. I shot him and watched him die."

"How?"

We both turned at that question. Larry stood in the doorway. Abigail struggled to sit up. I propped a pillow behind her to help.

"What do you mean, how?"

"I mean... and Abigail, if I may call you that? You did save my life, so I feel that puts us on a first-name basis. Can you tell me exactly where and how he died?"

Abigail thought about it for but a second then nodded.

"That seems to be the very least I can do," she said.

EIGHTEEN

"I WAS the lead investigator on one of his last... public kills. He took out an ADA in Chicago; we still don't know why, but he invaded her home and killed her, her husband, her mother, and the DA's three children. The kids were all under the age of twelve. He also killed two cops assigned to her family for protection. He cut them all up. The scene suggested he tied up the ADA and killed her family in front of her, then tortured her until she died. I've seen a lot of horrors. I'm a cop. But none of us had ever seen anything like that. Never. All I wanted to do was make him pay for that shit. Pay with his life."

Abigail motioned for water, and I helped her sip from a glass.

"What was her name, the ADA?" Larry asked.

"Tina Chavez. She was good, very good. I worked with her on a couple of cases. Gossip said she would end up as the new DA, mayor, or even President. She had that thing, you know? She walked into a room and took it over. When I saw what that... creep had done to her, done to her family, I wanted to be there to see him die."

"Why did she have police protection?" I asked.

"She was an ADA, a public face in pursuit of justice, and she'd already had several death threats for various cases she'd overseen. She had three RICO cases pending at the time of her death, among others. We looked into all of them but could not find a connection to Tolliver in any of them. If he'd been paid to kill her, we could not determine which party was responsible due to the sheer number of those who benefited from her death."

"But someone must have paid him for that," Larry said.

"Yeah, that's what I thought. A few of the brass felt he was showing off, showing us that he could hit cops and above whenever he wanted to. And it played to that part of the population that hates cops, so it was a... hero move to some. A huge middle finger to everyone trying to catch him. It looked exactly like something he would do. Looked.

"I couldn't put my finger on it, but it didn't feel like a thrill kill, which the experts said Munson specialized in. Sure, that element was there, no doubt. We knew he liked challenges and loved publicity, but something about this felt... even more deliberate. That there was a greater goal beyond that. I had no evidence to support that. None. Just my intuition that he didn't choose this family as a target. Someone else did. I was certain of that. But this was a multi-task force with bigger names calling the shots, and all I had was a sixth sense, nothing more.

"The investigation dragged on for months with no progress. We shut down the airports, bus, and train stations and had checkpoints at every highway, but we never saw a whisper of him. Nothing. We dug into Chavez's past and present cases and found no connection. Dead end."

Abigail took a deep breath and let it out. Glanced at me.

"Two things about this case stuck out for me, two things that no one had ever gotten a good answer for. One. Facial recognition. We have the best facial recog programs in the modern world, bar none. Our nation is first with that. They see through masks, makeup, hats, a ton. Of course, Tolliver wears disguises; he has to. But we should have tracked him despite that. But we could not. Why?"

I straightened up at that, an idea or a memory tickling in my brain, but I couldn't put a finger on what it was. Not yet. I noticed Larry lean forward, too.

"The other thing is Tolliver loved to climb. He loved high-floor home invasions. We knew he was an accomplished climber, both with ropes and without. The shrinks felt it was part of his process, part of what... turned him on about the... hunt, for lack of a better word. He wanted challenges and obstacles to the kill to make it worth it. That wasn't new. What was new was that Cruz and her family lived in the Daly Building, in the penthouse. Fifty stories above the city. Impossible to climb. He didn't even approach the lobby. Too many cameras and guards. He didn't climb the sheer glass outside; not only was that considered nearly impossible to do in the best of circumstances, but it was raining the night they were murdered. And cameras from surrounding buildings would have picked him up. Nothing.

"Yet, he appeared on the top floor, killed the two cops on guard, got into the home, and took his time killing the family. And he got out of the penthouse without being seen. Didn't come down by the elevator or stairs. Nothing. So how? No helios were in the area; they're all monitored by law enforcement, nor was there any place for one to land on that building. So, two mysteries before me. How did he avoid facial recog, and how did he get up there and down again?"

"That happened with Sylvia, too," I said. "He went out the window, five floors up, and I didn't see him climb up or down."

"Yeah, I remember," Abigail said. "But I believed he was dead, so you were the only logical suspect. I'm sorry."

"I understand. So how did you find him?"

"I decided to focus on the two areas that had no answers. Facial recognition and his high tower entrances. A buddy of mine, an ex-boyfriend, used to work for the Defense Department. An engineer, he designed things for them to use in a military capacity. The thing was, Tolliver couldn't fly there, right? Not even a drone could bring him in without triggering an alarm. All high rises have sensors for flying mechanical objects; if he'd flown a drone in, the motor would have triggered the alarm. He didn't parachute in or out. I asked my ex, and he knew right away what was up. But he couldn't say. Wouldn't. He did, however, point me in the right direction. A little tech shop called MACHINA, based right there in Chicago."

Larry leaned forward when she mentioned the name of the tech shop. I wondered about that.

"So I went down to the shop. I went after hours when there wouldn't be many people there. There were lots of security measures just to get inside. It was hard as hell to get them to open up. It was only after I shouted that I'd camp out in front of the place until a judge gave me a warrant that they finally opened up. That's when I knew they had to be dirty."

"How?" Larry asked.

"Because I had no probable cause for a warrant. None. I had a rumor from an ex who wouldn't even go on the record. No way I could get a warrant, and anyone with sense knew that. But they also knew all the city's cops were pissed about the ADA's death. They knew I could lie and get a warrant; they knew I'd get in if I wanted to. But they opened up to one cop rather than ten, and that's when I knew something was wrong. And if I hadn't been so hot, I would have waited until at least Daniel or a team got there. But I was pissed. I didn't want to wait. I was arrogant. I got in the face of the security team there, spoiling for a fight. They sensed that. Let me in."

Abigail coughed and leaned back.

"At the time, I thought I'd caught them with their pants down. I bullied my way into the offices and spoke to their security head, saying I'd received an anonymous tip that Tolliver had been using some of their tech. I wanted to see what they had to use to get a man to the top of a skyscraper without setting off alarms, and that if I didn't get it, the State AG would, and I wasn't leaving until I was satisfied.

"They looked at each other. A phone rang, and they agreed to let me in after they answered it. The moment I stepped inside the lobby was when the fertilizer hit the propeller. Tolliver was there. After they buzzed me in and I stepped foot inside, he appeared from the back and opened fire at me in the lobby. It was him. I saw him. His eyes, those were the eyes of a killer. I'll never forget it. I dropped and returned fire. He missed me but hit the two employees there, killing both.

"Tolliver disappeared through a back stairwell. I called it in and continued my pursuit. He didn't go down or out; he went up, firing at me from the stairwell. He also shot and killed anyone that he came across along the way: security guards, custodial staff, everyone. He turned that entire secure office building into a morgue.

"I figure he sniffed out someone had connected him to the place, and he went there to clean his trail. And I interrupted him in the middle of it. Later, it was discovered that most of the vics had been killed before I arrived. The CEO of the company was found in his office, throat slit. Munson had started his purge right before I got there."

"Good timing," Larry said.

"Good for me, bad for them and him. Or so I thought at the time. I kept going, firing at him whenever I had an opening. He was quick; I'd never seen anyone move like that. I knew where he was headed, though. He was going for the roof. I wasn't going to let him get away. No."

I glanced at Larry, who was as rapt as I was.

"I made it to the roof just after he did. He was trying to attach some gadget to his back; I'd later discover it was a solar-powered prototype of a stealth personal glider. One exclusively developed by MACHINA. It was what he used to get up in high places. But he had trouble getting it to work when I found him. I shouted at Tolliver to stop and drop his weapon. The official version is that he turned and tried to fire. I shot and killed him. He fell off the roof onto the pavement. That was the official version."

"And unofficially," Larry asked.

"Unofficially, he dropped the weapon and turned to face me with his hands up. And I didn't hesitate. I shot him dead. I emptied my pistol as I walked toward him and didn't stop until he went over the side."

"With all due respect," I said, diplomatic, "I dove into research about Tolliver after I left Chicago, and nothing was said about who shot him. It read that—"

"I know; I took my name off of the shooting."

"Why," asked Larry.

"I wanted to end him and then refuse to talk about how he died. I wanted him to die in a void of attention. And that's what I did. I shot him, did zero interviews, turned down multiple offers, and insisted my name be kept out of it. Allegedly for security reasons, as Tolliver had rabid fans, but the reality was, I did not want to make him even more famous in death. No one got any publicity from the shooting. No one. The official statement read that Tolliver died in a hail of gunfire from multiple officers. That's not true. I shot him. No one else. The departments crafted that statement at my request. Our entire department was credited with bringing him down."

Abigail coughed and turned away from us. "And now I have to accept the fact that not only did I NOT shoot the actual Munson Tolliver, I killed someone else. Murdered someone else, someone innocent. And I'm never going to live that down."

"I believe it's safe to presume the man you shot was hardly innocent," Larry said. "And I say that as a committed pacifist, mind you. He looked like Tolliver, yes?"

She turned back to us. "Yes. And his blood was red."

"But we know now it wasn't him. A double, a human double for Tolliver, was there as if waiting for you to..."

"Shoot to kill," Abigail whispered. "They knew I wouldn't arrest him, that I'd kill him first."

"The lab confirmed Tolliver's DNA," I said. "But if he had given them a DNA sample beforehand, it would have been simple, yes? They could have easily switched his DNA from the DNA from the actual body."

"But that would mean Chicago PD was in on this at the highest level. That they were in on the murder of an ADA, and—"

"And someone sent two officers to kill me and Daniel," I said. "Someone up high. They knew who killed Sylvia."

"So they set up a fake Tolliver to be shot by a cop," Larry said. "To make him invisible and more useful. And later, they had to kill the synthetic who showed up unexpectedly as a witness to one of his crimes."

"Yes, he was supposed to be dead when he killed my Sylvia. He wore a mask to hide who he was but didn't expect me to show up and to be able to... fight back. If not for me, she'd be just another murder victim in a city full of unsolved murders."

"The Tolliver I saw in the lobby of MACHINA wasn't a fake," Abigail said, sitting up again. "I'll never forget the look on his face. That was a killer. Not a double. I watched him kill the two guards. I watched him murder others. He was fast.

Brutal. The man on the roof? Not Tolliver, we know that now. But Tolliver was there. In the lobby, I did see him. He switched. It was planned."

Abigail coughed hard. Larry exchanged a look with me.

"There's a lot here to consider," he said. "But you need rest. Sleep now, and we'll continue this discussion later."

I could tell Abigail wanted to argue but had no energy. We left her to doze off. There was much to think over.

NINETEEN

ANXIETY NIPPED at the edge of my existence constantly now. I couldn't sit still. I couldn't stop the thoughts in my head from rolling and roiling. I knew my memory was no longer as precise as it once was, and I ruminated obsessively over everything I could remember about my life after Sylva died. I felt there was something in there that was key.

But I couldn't find it. I slept poorly but did recall a piece of information that might link to whatever it was I was trying to remember. I sought out Larry the moment I awoke. He was in his office at his computer. He looked as though he'd been up all night. The song THE GRAND ILLUSION blasted on his computer speakers.

"Hey Jacob," Larry leaned back, stretching. "Looks like you have something to say. What's on your mind?"

"You seem to doubt that there's a fix for our blood."

"I do. But it's one thing I'd be happy to be wrong about."

"Why do you doubt it?"

"Oh. Huh. Well, some of it is pure logic. It's not just a defining trait of synthetics, but THE defining trait. Sure, they fibbed about emotions, but that was never logical to begin with. You must feel pain to comply. Not having human emotion, that's the kind of corporate lie we've come to know and expect in terms of marketing. It makes the consumer feel better about what they bought, and that's all that matters. The blood, however, was designed with a specific purpose, so if it's reversible, which I hope it is, it's not going to be easy. It's core. Part and parcel of a synthetic's identity. Maybe it's ego, but I also like to think that if there were a way to reverse it, I would have found it by now. And I have not, sadly. But here I am."

"How much do you really know about synthetics?" I asked.

"Not to sound egotistical, but more than most. Why?"

"Did you know that synthetics are immune to facial ID scans?"

"I did, they... you... were designed that way. I can see where this is going. No, Tolliver is not a synthetic, not as far as I can tell. He likely had his face altered via surgery to avoid facial ID. That's more logical. And it's been possible, though not public knowledge, since synthetics were first introduced."

"Oh," I said, deflated. "I've met combat models and thought—"

"That he was built by the company as a weapon against their enemies, yes, I'd considered that, too. Like you, I researched Tolliver's past and career. It's very apparent someone did an internet scrub as best they could because there was so little information available, but Tolliver was indeed born human. Plus, I saw him. I saw him in action. He's not synthetic. Abigail winged him. I saw his blood. His blood was red. That's not possible with synthetics, and it has never been. I wish it were. It's something the movement has worked for from the very beginning.

"The good news is that I've been able to crack the encryption on the information we recovered from the hub, which meant nothing is stopping us from accessing it on the drive.

"The bad news is that it's not possible to copy. It's set up so that if someone attempts to copy it, it destroys itself, and an added problem is that it's a lot of data, and without context or knowing what we're looking for, it's next to hopeless to find what we're looking for in a reasonable amount of time. Too dense, too complex, and far too vast. It'd be like trying to find a specific cup of water in the ocean. It won't stop me from searching for the fix, but even with what I know, I can't say I'll be able to find it if it even exists. I'm trying, though. I'm trying."

"Larry, did Tolliver see you? Did he get a very good look at your face?"

"I'd have to say yes. I was next in line for the DNA check and eventual shooting, if not for Abigail."

"You can't stay here, Larry. He'll come looking for you. He hates loose ends, especially since Abigail was with you. He'll search for you both. You need to leave."

"And go where? Abigail cannot travel in her current state, and my child is due to be born in the next few weeks. Evie can't travel in her condition. It puts the baby at risk. It makes no sense."

"You're in danger. He'll eventually find you here. He'll kill everyone he can. Everyone."

"I know. I saw. But running changes nothing. And it's far harder to find me than you might imagine. Since getting involved with the movement, I've been most careful to cover my tracks, digital footprints, and everything. Running only draws attention. I've been doing this for a while now and am good at it. Plus, I have a community I know and love, who knows and loves me. I have my home, which is much safer than it looks, and my friends."

I took a breath and let it out. "Men... from this community... were coming to kill Evie. I heard them. They planned to rape and kill her, then frame me for it."

He sat back and exhaled. "I know, Jacob. I cannot express the gratitude I feel to you for saving her and me from that nightmare. It was a shock to hear it, and I'm still processing everything that's happened in the past twenty-four hours. I've known those men you stopped for years. Bewildering. But one cannot be a pacifist only when it's convenient. You have to be one when you're tested, too."

I was at a loss for words. But only for a moment.

"You mean to say that if Tolliver were here right now, ready to kill you, Evie, and your unborn child, you'd do nothing to stop him?"

"Untrue. I'd try to appeal to his humanity, long shot though that may be. It's what I was doing in the hub. I was the next to die, Jacob."

"Appealing to someone's humanity only works if they have humanity, Larry."

"It worked for Gandhi against the English."

"I did not work for the Mayans against the Spanish and Portuguese. And it won't work with Munson Tolliver or the Companion corporation. I think you know that."

Larry sighed, nodding. "I do. But as I said, this is who I am now."

"But Evie and—"

"Here's the thing, and this will be my last word. I was at a loss when I left medicine for private sector work. I didn't know who I was. I didn't even know what I was other than appetite and desire. All I did was consume distractions, express anger and rage, and hate myself. Then I met someone special. I met Evie. She changed me. Inspired me to be a better man. A humane one. If not for Evie, I would have been lost forever, a creature of appetite rather than a man with principles and purpose. I found a way to use the gifts I've been given to help others without compromising who I strive to be.

"If I pick up a weapon to fight, if I take a life out of anger or rage, then I am no longer the man Evie fell in love with, and I'd rather die than that happen. She knows that and feels the same. That's who we are. We cannot compromise our humanity to live in misery. We won't, Jacob. We cannot. I hope you understand."

"Does it compromise my humanity if I defend myself? Or if I defend Evie and you? Of course, I am a synthetic, so maybe I don't have any to begin with, which I accept. Did Abigail compromise hers when she saved your life?"

Larry sighed again. "Snark aside, of course, you have humanity; it's one of the many amazing things about you. No, I don't believe that your use of violence in the manner that you do, or what Abigail did, compromises your humanity in any fashion. I'm alive, and Evie's alive because of the both of you. I'm grateful. However, that kind of decision can only be made by the individual. You can act like that without compromising what makes you who you are. I know, based on my past experiences, that I cannot. I can't. And so I won't."

He smiled and turned back to his computer, focusing.

TWENTY

MY MIND WASN'T what it used to be. I used to remember everything. At least everything that I saw. I had total visual recall for as long as I could remember, right up until I woke up in Larry and Evie's home. The drugs must have damaged my mind. That and the physical abuse. Getting struck in the head multiple times cannot be healthy for the brain. It was, as Larry often said, only logical.

A few days passed by quickly, with Abigail recovering slowly but surely. Honestly, I felt as restless as an animal in a cage, but Larry and Evie did their chores and work with a smile. Arnold healed up and returned to his job, making the excuse that a cow kicked him in the arm to explain the sling.

There was usually a police car stationed not far from our home, too. I know it was meant to make Evie and Larry feel safe, but I could not help but suspect it was more to keep an eye on them and me. I had one more session to fix my aging issue, and then I'd be free and finished with it. We made a rare trip to town. I felt something amiss— like a target was affixed to our back. People watched us, friends and strangers alike. Larry maintained the new distrust of synthetic companions caused it. I wasn't so sure.

I didn't see Brent's injured buddies anywhere, nor did I expect to, but for one brief instant, I saw Brent exiting a bar as we drove by, glaring daggers at Larry and me. He knew, somehow, that we had hurt his friends. He knew Larry and I were responsible. I don't know if he realized that we knew what he had planned to do. I doubted it, but the truth was that I worried more about Tolliver than anything or anyone else.

Tolliver was in the area. I sensed it; I felt it. His presence blanketed the background of my every thought and emotion. Dread was an ever-present companion to my existence. He was close—very close.

Arnold and Larry completed my treatment, my final one, and it was while I was under that the whole story unfolded before me like a kaleidoscope. Even through the blinding headache, I felt inspired. There was something there in that story that was key. I had to find it.

IT TOOK me an entire day to recover from my session, but once I did, I hurried to Abigail's room. She sat in a wheelchair, staring out the window. Evie said she would walk eventually, but not without a considerable amount of physical therapy. Socrates, the cat, sat on the bed nearby and rolled on his back to show me his belly when I came in.

"If you'd have told me a year ago that today I'd be sitting in a chair, petting a cat and watching the birds in the trees out in the woods, I woulda told you, no fucking way," Abigail said. "But, well, here I am."

She reached over and scratched Socrates behind his ears. "Before this, I always hated cats, always. And now—what can I say? The big furry bastard broke me in and won me over."

Abigail made a kissing noise, and Socrates leaped off the bed and onto her lap, curling up. "Fuzzball."

"I need your help," I said.

"Hit me," she said.

"I'm sorry?"

"Hit me. Tell me what you need; it's an expression for chrissakes."

"Oh. Uh, last time someone said that to me, they meant—"

"I got it, I got it, it means I'm old. What's up?"

"I feel like I have an answer to some of what Tolliver is doing somewhere in my head, but I can't quite identify it. Like a—"

"Scratch that you can't itch."

"Yes. I feel I've seen or heard something important at some point, but I can't identify it. Not exactly. I don't know how to do so."

"Talk."

"I'm sorry?"

"Talk. Tell me everything," Abigail said. "From the moment you left Chicago until now, tell me everything you witnessed, experienced, thought, or even felt. Go over it with me, and we'll find out what it was. Talk. Omit nothing."

I blinked. "That's going to take quite a bit of time."

"I'm in a wheelchair with a fucking cat on my lap," she said. "What the fuck else do I have to do with my time?"

I took a deep breath and nodded. "All right. I'll tell you everything I can remember about my life as best I can."

And that's what I did.

ABIGAIL TURNED out to be an excellent listener. I would have never guessed that, but she nodded along, was quietly supportive, asked questions when necessary, and responded honestly to the awfulness of some of my experiences.

The death of Strawberry Fields moved her considerably, as she'd been in New York City when that all happened, but my adventures fighting in a box against other synthetics affected her the most. My tale of being forced to kill my own kind shattered something in her. After that part of my life was covered, we had to take a break due to her emotional response and because Evie brought us lunch. Evie asked no questions; she just smiled and shut the door behind her.

After eating, I returned to my tale and recounted my adventures in Stronghold, Raven Running Wolf's murder, Earth First, Lewis Yard, and my face-off with Munson. Doing that felt both exhausting and yet somehow therapeutic. After our lunch break, Abigail told me not to stop until I reached the end. She wanted the story fresh from me.

Once I finished, she held up her finger as if to say… wait. I did. It was nearly dinner time by then. Then she beckoned me with a finger and rolled out of her room. I followed her through the house until we arrived at what Larry called his brain-storming room. It was another office space but with a big holo board for writing.

"What are we doing here?" I asked.

"Write the names."

"Names?"

"People, places, and things, all the main names. Just the names, nothing else. Mainly the people. Start at the very beginning."

I nodded and used my finger to write "SYLVIA KIND" in bold letters on the holo-board, then "MUNSON TOLLIVER."

Inspiration hit after I wrote the third name. I gaped at it and glanced at Sylvia, who nodded. "You see it, don't you?"

"I do, now," I said.

"See what?" Larry said, appearing in the doorway. He looked exhausted.

"An important piece of our puzzle," I said.

"Glad one of us feels that way," Larry said. "I'm stymied on the boatload of data I've been sifting through. So what'd you find out?"

"First, Sylvia was killed by Munson once she discovered a name. Before she died, she told me to find that person and ask him why my blood was green. The name of that person was Larkin Finn. I never found Larkin Finn. However, by fate or fortune, he found me."

I turned and looked at Larry, who raised an eyebrow. "Uh, what do you mean by—"

"What I mean to say is— you're Larkin Finn."

TWENTY-ONE

LARRY DIDN'T TRY to deny it; he simply closed the door behind him and leaned against it. Sighed.

"*You never really understand a person until you consider things from his point of view... until you climb inside of his skin and walk around in it,*" Larry said, quoting TO KILL A MOCKINGBIRD. "I thought at some point you'd figure that out. I've hid for over a decade, and no one, not even Evie, knows who I once was," Larry said. "Nor will she. Ever. I buried that name. That information does not leave this room. Are we clear on that? She never finds out my former name. Never. Plus, there's another problem."

"What's that?"

"I don't know why Sylvia sent you to find me. That's one reason I never said anything. I'm out of my former life and have been out for a long time. I don't know what I have that Sylvia thought was of value. Or what Tolliver wants from me. I don't have anything of value for him."

"Who were you," Abigail asked, "before you became Larry Farmer?"

"Twenty or so years ago, I was one of the co-founders of PLUS ONE, which would eventually become COMPAN-

ION. It was myself and a few others who started the company."

"Adam Gilroy?" I asked, writing his name on the holo-board.

"Yes, he was one of them; there were others. How did you know the name Adam Gilroy?"

"Adam Gilroy was Munson Tolliver's first official victim."

"What? That can't be."

"Ten years ago. It was covered widely by the news. Most everything on that has been scrubbed by now, however."

"Ten years ago? I left Companion five years before that. I was completely off-grid at the time; I didn't follow any news at all then. You're telling me that Tolliver killed him ten years ago?"

"In public. In front of witnesses. In South Bend. Gilroy, like you, had just left Companion."

"Oh my god. I had no idea. That had to be some kind of message."

"Keep listing the names, Jacob," Abigail said. "We're onto something."

I did as she suggested. I wrote Adam's name, then his sisters. I followed that with Strawberry Fields.

"That place in Central Park?" Larry asked.

"No, a person. A synthetic person, I found out about our accelerated aging from her and the underground movement to Canada."

"In New York City? It's not a place but a person? Holy..."

"Was a person. Tolliver murdered her."

"The idea of an underground railroad was birthed in Central Park, New York City. It was also where data and information on synthetics were first collected outside of the corporation itself. It became a key hub for the movement."

"And Tolliver put a stop to that."

"So Adam leaves Companion, Tolliver kills him. Strawberry Fields becomes a central hub for synthetic information, and Tolliver kills her, too. Who else?"

"He was supposed to kill a woman named Raven Running Wolf. He was hired by a mining company backed by Frontier Capital and Companion. They wanted Raven't tribal land to mine a mineral needed to produce synthetics."

"A mineral? Curiouser and curiouser. That doesn't quite compute. Wait, Colton Cleveland?"

I'd just written that name after Lewis Yard. "Yes, he's one of the people who hired Tolliver."

"Another founding member from Plus One."

"Plus One?" Abigail asked. "Plus One was the name of Companion, originally?"

"Yes, but we became Companion when we absorbed two other companies. Plus One LLC joined CREATORZ, which was Jimmy Herschberg's venture, and another company called Red Harvest to become—"

"Red Harvest?" Abigail said. "Are you certain of that?"

"Uh, absolutely certain. The three companies became one."

"One of the men indicted in Tina Chavez's RICO case was Grant Cruz. He'd been an investor in Red Harvest early on," Abigail said. "That's a connection to Tolliver. They had Tolliver kill her to free up Grant Cruz or get him off the hook or something."

"Grant was a name I heard in Stronghold, too," I said. "He's part of Companion, one of those calling the shots, next to Colton Cleveland."

Larry leaned against the door. "One of the conditions of the merger, from Adam's end, was that Grant Cruz be divested from Red Harvest. Fired, in other words. Booted. Not part of the deal or partnership. His background was problematic.

"Simply put, he was a sociopath, and Adam refused to

work with him. They took him on after he and I left the company. So, somehow, Companion connected with Munson Tolliver and proposed a working relationship, yes? They pay him, and he makes their problems go away."

"Yes, he told me as much himself," I said.

"Which was so lucrative they even arranged to fake his death. And they've targeted those who they deem as threats to the company. But why Adam, why me? I left before synthetics were even public knowledge. I've been out so long I don't see how I could be a threat."

"You're running synthetics to Canada," Abigail said.

"Sure, but there are many of us involved in that, some doing much more than I am. Strawberry being taken out, that makes sense, but me? Only a few know of my involvement, and I have no power in the movement. Why would Sylva mention my name? Why would Tolliver be so intent on finding me that he's checking the DNA of anyone in the movement?"

"Sylvia asked me if I knew why my blood was green," I said. "That was her message."

"I know, but you answered that question earlier, Jacob. It's so we can tell them apart from humans. But I don't think that's why they're searching for me. I had nothing to do with that, and if I knew how to fix it, I would have by now."

"Maybe they, or someone, believes you can fix it?" I said.

Larry sighed. "Maybe. But I haven't the slightest idea how, not. Yet. I hope that I can find a way. I really do."

Nothing was said for a moment. I kept writing names. When I wrote H4711, however, Larry stopped me.

"What is that?"

"The mineral they were digging for. It's not the real name; it's code for whatever it is. Lewis Yard said they didn't use it in the beginning, but now they need a lot of it to make more synthetics. Because synthetics don't reproduce, they can't make any more of my kind without it."

"A mineral necessary for the creation of... that doesn't make sense," Larry said. "Wait. Holy crap. He didn't. But he must have. Shit!"

Larry ran out of the room. I realized that was the first time I'd heard him curse out loud. Abigail glanced at me, and we followed him.

TWENTY-TWO

WE FOUND Larry in his private office on his computer. Typing like a madman and staring at codes and numbers on the screen. He also booted up his holo-stereo, and the song ROCKING THE PARADISE played at high volume.

"So," Abigail said as she cruised forward in her wheelchair. "Care to explain?"

"Uh... oh, sorry. Um, the science is really dense, and it doesn't matter. I mean, it does, but it doesn't. I'm babbling, aren't I? Sorry."

He lowered the volume of the music, took a deep breath, and pushed his chair away.

"Long story short, not all of the founders of Companion were okay with the morality of creating life only to have it enslaved. A few of the founding members objected: Adam, Seth, Otto. They... we... wanted to use this creation for the good of humanity. We had the majority, but I saw the writing on the wall and bailed out early. I... was also dealing with a personal issue, and... that's primarily why I left. But I suspect Adam and a couple of others built a backdoor to our creation. That had been my private suggestion to Adam when I left the company. Apparently, he took my advice."

"Backdoor?" I said.

"A failsafe. In programming, they'll put something in that, if you default on paying your programmers, it's a time lock that freezes the program. For synthetics, something different. He made it so that, at some point, the process would cease to work. A tipping point. That happened; Adam built it in, somehow, and it jammed them up. They couldn't create them as they did previously. And they found a workaround with a new mineral, but if it's what I think it is, it's a very limited resource. In other words, they won't be able to create any new synthetics soon, if not sooner. At all."

"Holy shit," Abigail said.

"And then some," Larry said. "Next to fixing the blood color, this is massive. Adam was murdered after he left the company, apparently they thought they had all of his proprietary science in the bag. Then it hit a tripwire somewhere. They know the workaround is temporary. They can't make synthetics reproduce on their own. They know that sooner or later unless they undo whatever Adam did, they won't be able to make any more of them. They don't make more; they can't sell any more of them. Cripples the corporation."

"Which is why they're searching so hard for you," I said. "They don't want to kill you. They want you alive so that you can fix it."

"That's it," Abigail said. "That's why he checked everyone's DNA before he killed them. He needs you alive. They need you alive."

"But even if I could figure out how to undo what Adam did, I wouldn't," Larry said. "It would not be ethical."

"They would find a way to force you," Abigail said.

"I wouldn't," he repeated. "I won't help them, no."

"We all have vulnerabilities, Larry," she said. She glanced at the door in the direction of the kitchen. We could hear Evie singing as she prepared dinner. Larry paled.

"They know you're in the Woodstock area," I said. "I heard it from Strawberry's people. Tolliver knows it, too; it's why he came here. They know you're close. You can't stay here. Things are different now. You're not simply running synthetics to Canada. You represent to them billions and billions of dollars of future revenue. They'll stop at nothing when it comes to making you do what they want you to do."

"Tolliver will stop at nothing," Abigail said. "I saw what he did to Chavez and her family. Everyone breaks at some point. Everyone."

"I cede your point," Larry said. "But running doesn't change any of that. I've done the running thing. I did everything I could to distance myself from what I... helped create. It did no good. They can get me in Canada, too, as easily as anywhere else. I promised Evie I was done running, that I'd make her a home to live and stay in, and I'm not leaving it. This is... our home. I won't run. I won't work for them, and I won't run."

We heard a vehicle honk its horn as it pulled up the drive. Then, a few more cars followed and parked along the road facing Larry's farm. I counted at least ten vehicles. I noticed the patrol car had disappeared. A man climbed out of one of the trucks and walked up the driveway. He waved at the house.

It was Munson Tolliver.

TWENTY-THREE

"HELLO IN THE HOUSE!" Tolliver shouted. Larry and Abigail crowded next to me at a window, gazing at the sight before us. It wasn't good.

Men poured out of the other trucks and cars, all armed. They quickly circled the property. Many of them looked familiar.

"Those aren't all men; some are synthetic combat models," I said.

"Yes, it seems they have arrived with ill intent," Larry said. Evie joined us at the window.

Outside, Munson snapped his fingers and held out a hand. One of the men dragged Arnold out of a car and handed him over to Munson. Munson took out a vicious-looking knife, held it under Arnold's chin, and shouted at the house.

"Hello, are you home? Avon calling!"

"Do you have any guns in the house at all?" Abigail asked. "Besides my pistol, what do we have to defend ourselves?"

"We have some protection," Larry said, taking out his phone and tapping into it. The entire house locked up, with metal shutters over the windows and electronic locks on every door and opening.

"Public service announcement, attention! Unless you want to watch me filet your friend, you'd best come out and answer me! We've shut down your phones and internet and blocked all the roads. You're trapped. Come out, or I'll cut your pal's head off and stuff it in this mailbox!"

A light on the top of Larry's mailbox lit up and spat out a hologram of Larry, who spoke from the safety of his house using a remote control pad.

"So you must be Munson Tolliver," Larry's hologram said. "I've heard quite a bit about you over the past few months."

"And you are the infamous Larkin Finn," Munson said.

Inside the home, Larry sighed and looked at Evie. She smiled at him. Patted his arm.

"I know. I've always known you had a past. I didn't know what it was, but I knew it was there. It's okay. It doesn't matter to me who you were. I know who you are now."

Larry nodded, eyes full. He turned back to his phone.

"That name no longer means anything to anyone, Mr. Tolliver."

"I beg to disagree. I've been looking for you for quite some time, well over a year. Who knew I had you in hand just days ago, too? So close then, so very close. But here I am now. I need you to come out of your house, or I'm gonna gut your friend here."

"Based on your past exploits and pathology, you're going to do that anyway. That's what you do. You kill. You're not known for mercy."

"Sure, I'm not. But it's your company calling the shots, not me. They set the parameters here. You come out, I'll let him go. You come with us; we leave your wife, your unborn child, and your friend Arnold here, and they'll be safe and alive."

"Don't do it, Larry," Arnold said.

Tolliver sighed and cut Arnold along his jawline. Arnold screamed as blood dripped. "Hush, you. Can't you see we're negotiating?"

"See, that is not the act of a reasonable man," Larry's hologram said, "which makes one think that any negotiation would be fruitless. One cannot reason with someone who doesn't speak the language. If you wish for me to believe you'll let my friends and family live, you'll have to do better. Speak and act with reason and diplomacy. You have to earn some bargaining equity from me."

Tolliver blinked and smiled. "You are a clever one, aren't you? I find that satisfying, given how long I've pursued you. I like a worthy opponent. So, how would you suggest I earn said equity?"

"Simple enough. Just release Arnold," Larry's hologram said.

Tolliver laughed. "Oh, Larkin, I am not that foolish."

"Call me Larry. I don't mean to free him; I mean, send him in here with me. You have my home surrounded by what looks to be at least twenty armed men and synthetics. Send Arnold inside. I can stitch him up, we can continue our negotiation, and this way, I know you mean it when you say you'll let them live."

Tolliver appeared to think that over and snapped his fingers. Brent exited one of the vehicles and whispered into Tolliver's ear. I couldn't tell what he was saying to Tolliver, but my best guess would have been that it'd be about the area around Larry's home. More men fanned out.

"Hi, Brent," Larry's hologram said. "I wouldn't let Brent get too close, Mr. Tolliver, not if I were you. By my estimate, he's acquired at least three sexually transmitted diseases over the past year. He gets them faster than the MD app on his phone can clear them up."

Brent blinked, backed away, and then glared at the hologram. But he said nothing. Tolliver waved him away and sighed.

"Thing is, I quite enjoy cutting up people in front of their friends and family," Tolliver said. "It's one of my favorite things."

"Yes, I've heard that about you."

"I let him go in there with you; I lose that pleasure. What do I get in return?"

"You earn a bit of my trust. I'm not giving myself over to you unless I am absolutely certain my wife and friends will be safe. Sending Arnold inside is a step in that direction."

Tolliver thought that over for a moment. He nodded at Larry's hologram. "You know, you are very correct. I'm not speaking the language of reason and diplomacy. Not at all my native tongue. My language is one of power and brutality."

Tolliver took his knife and cut Arnold down the center of his belly, opening up his insides, which spilled onto the ground. Arnold howled in agony and horror. Tolliver kept cutting more pieces off of Arnold until the man finally died. Tolliver tossed the corpse aside. Even those few human men with him were aghast. Evie cried out and looked away.

"That's my native tongue. I don't have to earn shit with you, Finn. Nothing. The only thing you need to know is that if you don't come out, I'll come in and gut your wife just like I gutted this fish right here."

"You're a monster," Larry's hologram said. "Damn you."

"Who's the monster, the scientist who created Frankenstein or his ugly creation? You're the scientist who created life in a laboratory," Tolliver said. "I'm just a simple man who takes it, which humans have done to each other ever since they first appeared. Murder is part and parcel of humanity, Finn, and always has been. I'm not the damned here... you are, slick. Now come out of there. I want you and the skin to exit the home with your hands in the air. I don't care about anyone else inside, just you and Jacob. I know he's with you."

"Jacob will have to decide for himself," Larry's hologram said. "I'll need a few moments to discuss it with him."

"You get two minutes," Tolliver said. Larry's hologram blinked off.

TWENTY-FOUR

LARRY STUMBLED back from his control pad, shaken and pale. I reached out and put my hand on his elbow to steady him. I'd never seen him in this state, and it worried me.

"I can't believe he just... just..." Larry couldn't continue.

"That's what he does," Abigail said grimly. "He's a killer. It's who he is. You know that. Bargaining didn't work with him before, and it won't work now. You can't go out there or give yourself up."

"I agree with Abigail; you can't go out there," I said.

"But if I don't, he'll... come in and hurt Evie..."

"He will do that regardless," Abigail said. "We have two choices: fight or run. It's dark outside now. Can we make it to the forest without being seen?"

"No, we can't. I have alternate exits, but they have too many men surrounding us, and we won't be able to get enough distance, especially in Evie's condition. I should just surrender—" Larry said.

"No," Evie said, firm. "No, Larry. No."

He looked at her, but before he could argue, she held her hand to stop him. "No."

"I'll go out," I said. "Let me face Tolliver."

"He won't be satisfied with that," Abigail said. "He wants Larkin Finn, and Larry is Larkin Finn. You and me are just the gravy for him. I say we fight. My gun, do you still have it? Do you have any other weapons?"

"No. I can't do that," Larry said. "I made a promise, and..."

"No," Evie said. "Stop. Stop it, now. I know what you're thinking, Larry. You're worried that if you run or fight back, I will see you as the man you once were and not who you are. I won't. I know who you are, inside. I know you're a good man. I know you want the best for me and our baby. I know who you truly are, Larry."

Larry didn't move or speak for a moment.

Evie grabbed his forearm and pulled him close. "I know you're tired of running. I am, too. I don't care what happens to me as long as we're together. I could live next to you, and I could die next to you and be happy. But it's not just us any longer. I've never asked you for anything in our time together —never—just that you love me and allow me to love you. But I'm asking you to do something for me now. Please. Fight back. Not for me. For our child."

Larry swallowed and closed his eyes. Outside, Tolliver shouted that his time was up. Larry sighed and nodded, and a change seemed to flow over him. Larry opened his eyes, picked up the control pad, and activated his hologram.

"Mr. Tolliver," Larry said. "Must you make such a racket?"

"Cute," a projected image of Tolliver replied. "Are you coming out, or am I coming in?"

"I think... neither," Larry said.

"I will kill your woman and child! I promise you that!"

"So you've said. It's been pointed out that you're a man

with little regard for honor or morality, so rather than make things easy for you, in light of the murder of my good friend, no. I won't come out. And it's doubtful you'll make it to me. It won't be easy for you to get inside. I built this entire facility. We can last for a long time here. You, however, cannot. You may have until daybreak before I find a way to get hold of the State Troopers, but rest assured, I will. You don't know me, Mr. Tolliver, do you?"

"I know enough to—"

"No, you don't really know who I am. Let me tell you something. I'm very smart. Smart enough to rig this whole homestead. Smart enough to open comms that you've blocked. Smart enough that I designed some of those synthetics you have running around helping you. I'm smarter than you and smarter than the people who hired you to find me. I'm smart enough that they want me alive."

He leaned forward, and his face seemed to change. He grew very cold and distant, yet somehow feral, too.

"You killed my friend and threatened my wife, Tolliver," Larry said. "If the company values me more than you, don't you think they'd grant me your head on a platter if I but asked? I think they would. If I were you, I'd run— as far away from this place as you can while you can."

The hologram Tolliver grinned. "So the stories I've heard are true. You can be a cold bastard when you want. Nah, Finn, they need me; they need my brutality to force you into compliance. For them."

"They were never that smart to begin with, Tolliver. You're smart enough on your own to recognize that. Run while you can."

"Heh. Nope. I enjoy this shit, my man. I love a smart scrap. I don't know you, but they do. They know you. They profiled you. They know how to push your buttons. And they gave all that intel to me. I'm the big bad middle finger that does the fucking pushing of said buttons. Let the game begin, Finn!"

Larry clicked off the comms. "I hate being called that."

TWENTY-FIVE

LARRY MOVED FAST AFTER THAT, barking orders at Evie that I didn't quite understand, not at first. Later, I'd understand he was prepping for an attack and that it was something he'd put thought into long before I'd ever arrived at his home.

Larry went to his office, sat at his desk, and began typing fast onto one of his consoles. Machine noise hummed, and I heard shutters close somewhere else in the house. He barely noticed Abigail and me following him, and only when it became apparent we were staring that he snapped out of it.

"They've blocked communication, online and off, but I'm not without resources. They'll struggle with cutting the power off here, however, given how I set up the solar. Given time, I can get through. How much time we have, though, I cannot say. It depends on how much destruction they're willing to do to get inside, which I'd estimate is quite a lot. They will eventually break in. But it won't be easy.

"The windows and doors of this home are embedded with titanium and far stronger than they look. They are also protected with volt-shields, among other things. This place looks like a farmhouse, but everything is reinforced and strong enough to withstand direct gunfire, grenade blasts, and many other destructive tools they may have at hand. Just because I am... was... a pacifist doesn't mean I don't believe in preparing for the worst. Speaking of which, Abigail, I presume you can use this better than I can."

Larry opened a drawer. Inside lay Abigail's pistol and ammunition. She wheeled over and grabbed the weapon, loading it quickly.

"There's a shotgun in the back hallway that hasn't been used in years, but it will come in handy. I used to be pretty good with it. I don't have any other firearms here, Jacob. However, I have some thoughts on how we can defend ourselves. I'd appreciate it if you could watch Evie for me, Abigail, while Jacob helps me."

Abigail nodded and glanced at me. She didn't speak; she just touched my arm as though I were her comrade-in-arms, which now seemed I was. Life was interesting, to say the least. She rolled her wheelchair out of Larry's office.

I sensed something else, another reason Larry had sent Abigail out, so I waited as he typed away. Finally, he sighed, pushed his chair back, and looked at me.

"Can you handle the cold hard truth?" Larry asked.

"It's my preference."

"I did good work; this entire home is basically a fortified panic room. However, they shut down our communications very efficiently. I don't know if I can break through in time. Sooner or later, they'll find a way inside—faster if they brought along an EMP, which let's presume they did. It's what I would do.

"I have an exit hatch, but it only goes as far as the greenhouse. Plus, Abigail won't make it through the exit tunnel, not in her chair or condition. And Evie cannot really run, either. You or I could possibly make it, but not them."

"We're not leaving them," I said.

"I'm not, no. I can't and won't. But I estimate we have three hours, at the most, before they crack their way inside. Less than an hour if they use an EMP. So they're coming in. That's inevitable. You've killed before. You're not going to have any problem doing it again?"

"No."

"Good. Our only advantage is that they need me alive if our hypothesis is correct, and I believe it is. They want you alive, too, or I presume the company does, and they'll want to leave Evie alive to use as leverage against me. Abigail, no."

"Tolliver will kill me if he gets the chance. And I'll definitely kill him the moment I can."

"That's what I wanted to talk to you about. Take this," he handed me a thumb drive. "Don't lose that, whatever you do. Once my house is breached, all the data and drives I have will destroy themselves. That drive, that's all that's left—my life's work. If anything happens to me... you'll take Evie out of the tunnel once they break in, and you'll get her to our friends in Canada, where it's safe for her and our child. As long as I'm alive, they'll never be safe."

"You want us... me... to leave you and Abigail here?"

"If we can't kill them all, that's the only remaining option. Statistically, we won't be able to survive an invasion here, even with all of my modifications. It's me they want the most. They won't stop until they have me or I'm dead. They want you, but they need me. It's the end of the road for me here, one way or another. But it is possible you can get Evie somewhere safe."

I didn't take the drive. I simply stared at him.

"It was you, wasn't it?" I said. "There were many involved in creating my kind, but you were the... brains behind it all. It was your idea, to begin with—to create artificial life. You."

He didn't answer one way or another; he just offered a wan smile and another quote from TO KILL A MOCKING-

BIRD: "*The one thing that doesn't abide by majority rule is a person's conscience.*"

"Why?" I asked. "Why did you do it? You thought that creating and enslaving artificial life would help humanity?"

"Honestly, I never thought about humanity, not even once back then," he said. "I only wondered if I could do the impossible. That's why I did it—because it had never been done before, and I could. I was... very different then. I... was consumed by achievement and nothing else. Once I did it, once I achieved the impossible, I was at a loss. I didn't know who I was or what I wanted. I thought once I achieved something no one else had ever done, I'd feel... satisfied. I didn't. I had more money than I could ever spend, and still, I was miserable. As miserable as I was when I began. So, I walked away from it all. Traveled the world. Nothing changed for me until... I met her."

He looked away as if embarrassed by his emotional reaction.

He pushed another drive at me. "If there is an answer to the problem of your blood, it'll be in here, the data from the hub; take this and the drive with all my work and give it to someone who can maybe fix this mess I... created."

He left the drives on his desk, stood, and opened another cabinet. "I don't have any more firearms, but I do have these, which I think might be of some use."

He pulled out an expensive hunting bow and a quiver of sharp-pointed hunting arrows. "This was a gift from a friend, long ago, that I have never used, but now is likely the time to break it in."

Numb, I hung the quiver and bow on my back. Larry rooted a bit more in his closet and came out with a samurai sword in a sheath. It was old and heavy, and the blade was extremely sharp.

"I got this in Japan, of course, when I craved such things in my youth. It's an artifact of another era, but it works."

I took the sword from him and hung it on my back. He glanced at the data drives on his desk, then at me, and sighed. He picked them up and held them out to me. I just looked at him.

"I'm sorry, Jacob. I know you may have hoped for something or someone more in terms of meeting your creator, but the truth is, I was always a flawed man who lived in his head. Without Evie, it was easy for me to forget about others. I've pretended to be a real human for years, to the point I nearly believed it myself, until now. But now, I know. I know the real monster, and it's not my creation. It's me."

A blast outside rocked the home, followed by another. Both shook the foundation of the building. I realized that there was nothing more that could be said. I took both data drives from Larry, stuck them into my pocket, and ran out to the living room.

ANOTHER BLAST HAMMERED against the back door as I exited Larry's office. I also heard someone cutting steel somewhere. Evie exited a room carrying two backpacks, followed by Socrates.

The home's foundation rumbled again. Larry hurried out of his office, grabbed Evie's backpacks, and tossed them to me. Abigail rolled into the living room, checking her pistol. Another massive shake of the building's foundation, and the power went out.

"EMP," Larry said. "Just as I thought. Come on, this way, we have very little time now. Don't stay in the tunnel; it's not sturdy enough, and if they blast the house like I think they will, the tunnel could collapse on you."

"Tunnel. Wonderful. What about you?" Abigail asked.

"Don't worry about me. Evie, remember the generator. Once you turn that on, get out of there fast, promise?"

She didn't answer, just nodded, her face tight. Larry led us to the kitchen, moved the refrigerator, and exposed a trap door. He opened it and gestured for Evie to get on the ladder leading down. She grabbed him in a fierce hug, kissing him. Larry had to pry her off. Tears in her eyes, she fought back, but eventually, he got her to go down the trapdoor.

"Always remember," he said. "I love you, always."

"Always and forever," Evie said in return.

It hit me: She knew he wasn't continuing onward with her. She knew that he'd decided to stay behind. She knew and didn't argue or fight it; she accepted his sacrifice. Larry picked up Socrates and handed the cat down to his wife. Once she took the animal, she grabbed Larry's hand and squeezed it hard.

"Always," Evie said.

Then she disappeared. I looked at Abigail, who shrugged.

"I'm not going down that hole, Jacob," she said. Uh-uh, it's not gonna happen. He lost me at the tunnel. I get claustrophobic in tight spaces. And even if I didn't, even if I wasn't in this chair, I don't think I'd go. I'm spoiling for some blood, and I mean to get it. Larry, you go on, be with your wife. I'll hold them off while you go."

"No, Abigail, I can't. They want me; this is where they'll find me, one way or another. This is my Waterloo. Jacob?"

I dropped the backpacks down the trapdoor opening. I hopped on the ladder, careful not to catch the bow and sword on my back, but I stared up at them both before I descended.

"Larry, I'll protect Evie with my life. That's my word to you. I hope your kind never knows the torment you put upon the lives of mine. Playing doctor-savior in the woods to stray souls in need in no way makes up for the horror you birthed."

"I never thought it would, to be honest. Someday, Jacob, I hope you'll discover for yourself what it's like to create life," Larry said.

"I'll be lucky to live until tomorrow as it is. Abigail, for what it's worth, I consider you an exceptional human being," I said.

Abigail didn't speak, but her eyes filled. Larry grimly closed the trapdoor above me and dragged the refrigerator back over it.

TWENTY-SIX

IT WAS DARK, but Evie cracked open a glow stick ahead so I could see. I followed her to a small equipment room. She put the cat on the floor and flipped switches on a machine. Above us, somewhere, I heard Abigail's pistol fire. Abigail was putting up a good fight, I thought. I expected no less from her. Evie wiped tears from her face.

"Backup generator," she said. "One of Larry's creations. If I get the power back on, it may give them more time."

Evie pulled a massive lever, and the generator started. The lights came on as the house powered up again but with limited energy. Music blared from speakers; I recognized the song. DOMO ARIGATO, MISTER ROBOTO by Styx. I'd listened to him play this one often. Now, it covered our escape. Evie led the way further into the tunnel.

Gunfire echoed in the night air above. Shotgun blasts accented the pistol fire. Larry was now involved in the gun battle. The gloves of pacifism were completely off now.

With only the light of a single glow stick to navigate by, I couldn't make out much, but Evie seemed to know where we were going. She sobbed as she hurried along, finally arriving at a ladder. She pointed and whispered to me, "It comes out inside the greenhouse."

I nodded and set my pack down. Then, I carefully climbed the ladder to a trapdoor. I unlocked and opened it as quietly as possible. I noted I was inside the greenhouse just as Evie had said, specifically under a table plot of baby tomatoes. Everything in this building was still dark, but I could see lights and flashes from the house not but fifty yards away.

I did not see anyone directly outside the greenhouse, which boded well for our escape. Evie handed me the backpacks. I put one on, set the other aside, and helped Evie out of the tunnel. She stopped me before I could close the trapdoor. She clicked her tongue, and the cat Socrates quickly climbed up the ladder and hopped out.

I closed the trap door. We crouched under the table. The cat rubbed against me as I pulled out the bow and notched an arrow. The hunting arrows had wicked-looking, razor-sharp heads on them.

Staying low, we padded out from under the table and stopped before we got to the exit door. Men stood right outside the greenhouse, speaking in low tones. I couldn't tell if they were human or synthetic. Evie grabbed my hand, pulled me close, and whispered.

"Jacob, can you do what you did the other night with Brent's friends to these men?"

"I promised Larry I'd get you out of here and keep you safe," I whispered. "If I leave you here, then..."

"Please, Jacob. If we don't try to save them like they're saving us, what kind of people are we? Please."

I looked at her. When I attacked the two waiting rapists, I had the element of surprise in my favor. They were armed but didn't know I was close. This situation, however, meant facing twenty to thirty heavily armed men and synthetics, most with some training, plus seasoned serial killer Munson Tolliver. I had a bow and a few arrows, plus a samurai sword.

My odds were not great. Not even good. Plus, I'd promised Larry that I'd get Evie out safely. I'd be risking her life by trying to save Larry and Abigail. Sensing my hesitation, Evie put her hand on mine, eyes pleading. This woman had changed my soiled bedclothes, nurtured and fed me, babied me when I was sick, and never once complained. I could not say no to her. I nodded, slid my backpack off, and notched an arrow into the hunting bow.

Evie tapped my shoulder, indicating I should wait a moment, and dug into one of the planter's boxes. She pulled out a handful of dirt and rubbed it over my face, giving me natural camouflage. After she finished, she pulled me in and kissed my cheek.

"Thank you," she whispered. I patted her shoulder and slipped out of the greenhouse door. Lights flashed from the house, but they were dim enough to create more shadows and chaos rather than illumination. I spotted two groups of men on different sides of the house using a drill on the shutters. They'd already removed one set.

I noted dead bodies around the back door, which meant Larry and Abigail were able to fend them off before the power came back on. Movement dotted the shadows everywhere, which meant men surrounded the entire farm. MISTER ROBOTO blasted from inside.

I had to decide the best strategic course of action. If I attacked now and drew them away from the house, they would know I was outside; they would search for me, which might lead them to Evie. I needed a different distraction. I slipped away from the greenhouse and made my way toward the front of the home. Before I got too far, two men spotted me. I shot one with an arrow before he could shout.

It hit him in the throat, and he fell, choking on his own blood. I moved fast toward the remaining man, who fumbled his weapon. Before he could aim and fire, I elbowed him in the nose and throat, putting him down for good. Both men I'd killed were human, I saw. When I spotted a flash-bang grenade on one's belt, I knew my plan. I grabbed it quickly, but I heard more men trooping in my direction before I could take their weapons. I dived into the darkness quickly. They found the bodies and immediately went on high alert, shouting for Tolliver.

I rolled away into the shadows, making my way to Larry's truck. It was a classic truck, decades older than other vehicles, and a hybrid vehicle that ran on both gasoline and electricity. Larry's father had owned it. I know he kept it for so long as one last reminder that his father and I hoped he'd forgive me for what I was about to do.

I opened the gas cap, activated the grenade, and tossed it inside the truck tank. And then I ran. I ran away fast. As I did, more men spotted me and gave chase. Three of them reached the truck right when it blew up in an orange ball of fire. It lit up the night. I knew Larry would hear it and perhaps take heart. I hoped.

I ran behind the barn, the bow ready. I shot a sentry, killing him instantly, and then fired more arrows at the men attempting to break into the house. I killed at least three of them. I knew two were synthetic from their blood. I didn't know where Tolliver was at that moment, which worried me. It made sense that he'd send the combat models in to secure Larry and Abigail, and they would take losses on the home invasion. It stood to reason he'd let the cannon fodder do what they do.

But what would Tolliver do? I couldn't see an answer.

A bullet zinged near me. I dodged into the shadows again, firing another arrow in the direction of the shot. I didn't see it hit, but I heard it. I ran for the back toward the greenhouse. I heard Evie scream and ran harder. Four men searched the greenhouse, and one of them hauled Evie by her arm toward the door. I recognized the man. It was Brent Barker and some of his buddies. I fired more arrows, hitting and killing two of them, wounding another, and leaving Brent still standing. He held Evie close, and I didn't trust my aim.

"You!" Brent screamed.

He raised his pistol to fire at me, but before he could pull the trigger, Socrates leaped at him, scratching and clawing at his face. He dropped his weapon and fought with the cat. I aimed an arrow at him, but before I could kill Brent, another man ran at me, pointing a firearm. I buried an arrow in his eye. It was my last one.

I threw the bow down and sprinted toward Brent, still some distance away, battling with Socrates as Evie lay in the dirt near him. I'd never seen Socrates even hiss at anyone, much less turn into the destructive ball of furry murder he'd now become. Blood streamed down Brent's jaw and chest as Socrates howled in fury.

Brent finally tore the cat off his face and threw it at the greenhouse. Socrates wailed as the creature crashed through the glass. Brent saw me and dived for his pistol. He reached it and aimed, stopping me in my tracks.

"Hah! I got you, you fucking rim! Hey! I got the skin and the girl back here! Hey, boss-man, I got your rim right here!"

I stood a good twenty yards away from him. Too far. There was no way I could reach him before he could shoot me or Evie. He reached his feet, yanking Evie to hers, and kept calling for Tolliver. I glanced at the house, at least fifty or sixty yards away.

The shutters of the living room window suddenly opened. Larry stood in full view, holding a remote in his hand. Abigail was nowhere to be seen, nor could I recall hearing her pistol firing recently. In her condition, she'd likely already gone down.

Men surged toward the house, and a few more headed for Evie and me. Larry saw that, saw us, nodded, and held up the remote. He mouthed the words, "I love you," to Evie.

I shouted for Evie to get down and dived into the dirt. Larry gave us a little wave and pressed the remote. The entire house blew up in an orange cloud of fire. Evie screamed as her home and husband disintegrated before our eyes.

TWENTY-SEVEN

DEBRIS AND ASH rained down upon us. Evie sobbed and sobbed. The blast had taken out the men closest to the house and those running toward us. Larry's last attempt to help us escape killed most of the attackers and I wasn't going to let him die in vain. I scrambled to my feet and ran to Evie.

I reached Brent just as he stood back up. I kicked the pistol out of his hand, spinning it into darkness. He threw a roundhouse punch that I blocked. I back-handed him hard enough to put him on his butt.

He sat there in shock at what I'd just done. I could see it written on his face. I stepped toward him to finish him off but stopped when I heard snarls from the bushes. Two sets of animal eyes glowed in the darkness.

Zeus and Athena. The two massive cats attacked Brent before he could react. They both bit into his neck and face, going for the jugular. Brent flailed but was no match for the felines. Together, they ripped his throat right out. I watched him bleed to death before me.

I helped Evie to her feet. She cried so hard she could barely walk. I carried her weight toward the greenhouse. Socrates limped out, alive but bleeding. He looked at us, blinked, and then joined his parents by the dead body of Brent Barker. Evie and I watched them lick their offspring, then disappear into the woods.

Before I could enter the shattered greenhouse, a man shouted. Three synthetic combat models rushed toward us. They had pistols, but I knew somehow, somewhere in my soul, that they were tasked with bringing me in alive, which gave me a significant advantage. My hunch proved true when they holstered their weapons and pulled out Tasers. I leaned Evie against the greenhouse and unsheathed the samurai sword on my back.

The first Taser wires blasted out. I cut them in two. The two other synthetics also fired their Tasers, and I also cut those wires before they landed on me. They pulled out batons next and attacked. I did not take any more time with them than necessary. I cut one's arm off, the head of another, and the third, I impaled right through his heart.

Green blood splashed everything. The surviving synthetic held his remaining hand against the stump of his shoulder where his arm once was, slipping into shock. I didn't wait for that. I cut his head off. Laughter echoed in the shadows.

"You are just perfect," Tolliver said as he strolled out of the flickering shadows. "I could not have created you better, myself. I needed someone like you in my life to make it more interesting. And you have. There's but one being who has survived a fight with me. That's you. And you've done it more than once. It's a bit scary."

Tolliver stopped a few yards away. I noted he carried no firearms.

"I had twenty-five men here, ten real humans, fifteen combat models, and you and your friends killed every swinging dick I had here. I must say, killer to killer, that I am impressed. But guess what, you reached the final boss."

Tolliver reached behind his back and pulled out two sharp machetes, hefting one in each hand. He winked at me.

"You and me, blades versus blade. It's a dream come true. I can't remember the last time I felt this nervous or even if I ever have," he said. "I have to tell you. I kind of love it. It's exciting."

"I thought you were supposed to take me alive."

"That was the mandate, yes. But I was always going to kill you. I have to. I work with Companion, but I don't work for them. They'll be pissed Larkin Finn is dead, I'm sure, but who'd thought he'd commit suicide? Wasn't in his profile. Then again, neither was love, marriage, or fatherhood, so that shows you how much the shrinks don't know."

"He's dead because of you. So is Abigail, too."

"Yeah, I saw her inside the house as well, taking shots at my men. She fought well right until the very end. Maybe I underestimated them both. Never put either of them as capable of making that kind of sacrifice. I guess bringing you two alive into the company would be of some solace to them, but I ain't in the business of solace, as you might remember. I'm in the business of murder. My one true love. They'll have to settle for your head after I remove it from your shoulders."

"Not if I take yours first."

"Hah! I love it. You're shit-talking now. Listen to you. You've come a long, long way, rim. You're no longer just a bag of skin with a few dance moves. Uh-uh. You're something much more exquisite and gorgeous."

"And what would that be?"

"Dangerous. Lethal. A murderer like me. Your body count is commendable. It's near mine, which is saying something. It will be my crowning achievement when I finally kill you, Jacob. There's never been any human like me, ever, and never been any plastic like you. Two perfectly designed opposing forces. We're destined to do this."

And that was when the real battle began.

TWENTY-EIGHT

TOLLIVER CIRCLED ME, his eyes bright and wide. He did love this, I saw, and didn't hurry himself in the slightest. I took a deep breath, closed my eyes, exhaled, and remembered the classic film THE SEVEN SAMURAI. I'd watched it a few times, and the swordsmanship featured therein was excellent. I'd need those moves. I'd need to focus. I had it in mind now. I felt clear. I opened my eyes, now in a perfect stance, my blade held high. Evie watched us both, her eyes wide.

"Afterwards, what will I do with the woman?" Tolliver asked. "Do I show her some favor, give her a small taste of my brutality, or put her out of her misery right away? Hmm, decisions, decisions."

I noted that he was attempting to anger me, to make me emotional, and, therefore, less efficient in combat. I knew this from my days on the box-fighting circuit. It was a common tactic. I decided not to play, not yet. I'd fought him before and lost. I couldn't lose again.

Tolliver feinted in at me. I didn't fall for it. He feinted again, followed by a slicing cut that nicked my eyebrow. I'd seen it coming but moved too late to parry it. Green blood dripped down my cheek. Tolliver chuckled. Kept circling.

"First blood is mine, skin."

I feinted at Tolliver, then slashed. He parried it and countered with his other blade. I blocked that one, and sparks flew from our colliding blades. He stabbed, and I dodged, cutting him along his cheek. Red blood dripped down his face and neck now.

I didn't wait, however, and threw a kick at his thigh, one that connected. He didn't care for that and slashed at my chest, cutting it. It was a shallow cut but a bloody one nonetheless. He stabbed at my leg, and I barely slipped the strike.

"Piece by piece, bit by bit, I'm taking you home, rim," he said. "I'm taking you home with me in a fucking bag, boy."

I visualized an offensive move from a film I'd seen long ago, faked upward, down, and finished by stabbing straight for Tolliver's heart. He crossed his machetes before himself, trapping my blade before it could pierce his chest. He grinned.

"Predictable. That's what you are, skin. Everything you know you got from the movies, kid, and that ain't gonna be enough. You don't love the killing like I do. It's what will be your end."

He twisted both his wrists and wrenched my blade away, slinging it over my head and into the grass. I knew it right then and there. I was dead. He was too good with those blades, much better than I was. He put the edge of one machete under my chin.

"I win, skin, as I always knew I would," he said. "You're mine."

"No!" Evie screamed. She stood, holding a pistol she'd taken from Brent's dead body. "No! I'll kill you!"

Tolliver slowly turned toward her, one eyebrow raised. "You'd kill me? You?"

"Back away, or I will kill you!"

"Ah, I see. I back away, and you let me live, yes?"

"Just back away! Back off!"

I wanted to tell her to fire immediately, just to shoot him. Then I saw how much her hands shook. She feared hitting me at this distance. And added to that, she'd never taken a life, any life. Tolliver recognized it, too, and kicked me in the belly before I could say anything. I fell to my knees; the wind knocked out of my body.

Tolliver turned to Evie, machetes loose at his sides. "I don't think I want to back away. I think I want to take you right here. So, that means you're going to have to shoot me, girl."

"I'll do it!"

Before she could squeeze the trigger, Tolliver kicked some burning debris at her head, causing her to scream. She fired wide and away, up into the night sky. Tolliver leaped at her and knocked the weapon away with the flat of his blade. He howled in triumph and raised his machete high to kill Evie as she screamed. Before he could connect, however, I had found my sword and blocked his strike with a hard clang of steel.

"No," I said.

I kicked him in the gut, and he stumbled away from Evie. He quickly regained his balance and swiped at me. I blocked it. He whirled both blades in a figure-eight pattern, his eyes glinting. The house fire burned even brighter, and smoke and ashes floated between us.

"So you got a bit more fight in you, Jacob? That's good. I like that. I don't want this to be too easy. I want the challenge. I want this to last. I'm gonna cut the tendons in both of your legs and make you watch as I cut her to pieces. It's not enough to kill you. I want you to suffer."

He attacked again, employing multiple strikes at me. I blocked and parried each one, breathing deeply and easily. I talked as I fought.

"Suffering? You think you can show me suffering?" I said. "You haven't seen what I've seen. You haven't experienced the life of a slave. You don't know suffering, pain, agony—you know them, but you don't know them as intimately as I do. You know only the joy of causing pain, not taking it."

I cut twice, up and down, and began varying my attacks. He got serious and moved faster than I remember anyone else ever moving. We lost ourselves in a whirl of blades and blows. He WAS better at this than I was; I recognized that. He loved killing; he loved every part of that, and that joy infused his every action. I was desperate to live. He lived to kill. That meant I couldn't defeat him, not fighting as I was.

However, out of the corner of my eye, I caught a look at Evie, sitting on the ground, a shocked look on her face and her hand on her belly. All three cats, Socrates, Zeus, and Athena, milled around her in a protective cone, surrounding and shielding her. And I remembered that I wasn't only defending my life. I wasn't only defending Evie's life. I wasn't just fighting against Munson Tolliver.

I was fighting FOR something.

I fought for humanity. I took joy in fighting for humanity. I flashed back to all the best people I'd met on my travels, synthetic and natural, some names I'd never know, some with names I'd never forget. Every face that had ever shown kindness and empathy for me, every single one I could see in the flickering shadows of the fire.

They were there, the ones long since dead, like Sylvia and Daniel, and those hopefully still alive, like Toots and Mick. I battled for them and heard them cheer me on. Every person I ever cared about or who cared about me stood there in the night at my side in support, even Larry and Abigail. I saw them; I saw them all.

My mind cleared with joy.

Tolliver cut me again on the chest, then nearly speared my head. I rolled under his thrust, came around behind him, and nicked the back of his knee. He twirled both machetes, eyes furious, no longer toying with me. He wanted to end it. I could smell his desperation. I liked it.

I no longer cared about my own life. I only cared about Evie and everyone else's. That was the key, I realized. To live and fight for life.

I feinted high, went low, and then back high again, the same move I'd made earlier, aiming for his heart. As he'd done before, he brought his machetes up to trap my sword, but my blade wasn't there this time. I faked him out and went high to his throat instead.

I stabbed him in his Adam's apple and left it there, the point of my sword piercing all the way through and out the back. He fell to his knees, gagging on blood, unable to move, his spinal cord also severed.

"I hope you found that challenging enough."

Tolliver blinked, wishing to speak but unable to.

"I'm a killer, but not like you. I long for a day where I don't have to kill anyone ever again. A day when my kind is free."

I stared at him as the life slowly ebbed away from his body.

TWENTY-NINE

WE WERE STILL twenty miles away from the Canadian border when Evie's water broke just before sunrise. I pulled over and prepared to deliver Evie's baby. She had books on how to do it, and I read them as fast as possible, but this would be the first childbirth I'd ever witnessed.

I'd left Tolliver where he lay outside Larry's destroyed farmhouse. I did not leave, however, until certain Munson Tolliver was dead and gone for good. I grabbed both backpacks, the bow, and some arrows, but no guns. I left the samurai sword jammed into Tolliver's neck. I figured Larry would appreciate it if he were still alive.

We took one of the trucks the invaders had driven and hit the highway for Canada. With some luck, we'd make it there before daybreak. We had new passports with our pictures on them that Larry had created for us. He'd also given us contact names and numbers for fellow members of the free-Companion movement located where we were headed; he'd prepared everything for us.

Socrates didn't journey with us. We left it with its parents, Zeus and Athena, after Evie had treated the cuts Socrates had suffered. Evie called Socrates to the truck, but the cat didn't follow. It wanted to stay, and Evie recognized that. They watched us from the forest.

Evie stitched up and tended to my wounds. I'd have to look human, after all, and her skill as a nurse was unrivaled. Once we loaded up and I began driving, she cried silently and didn't stop until it became clear the baby wouldn't wait until we reached our destination.

I pulled over and made Evie as comfortable as possible in the back seat of the big truck. I kept as calm as I could under the circumstances. It did not take long; the baby came out fast —a girl, beautiful and loud. Every notable experience I'd had in my short life, from my first kiss, first fight, the first time I drank, the first time I experienced intimacy, nothing compared to being present as life was born. Nothing.

After it was done, I wrapped the baby in a towel and handed it to her mother, who hugged her close to her breast and fed her.

Evie said, "We're going to name her Finn."

I didn't speak, but I felt that was the perfect name for that beautiful girl. This birth was... unique, special, and one-of-a-kind. A lot of messy blood is involved in any childbirth, and this one was no different in that regard, except for one significant thing.

All the blood spattered all over the back seat was green. Evie's blood, and the blood of her baby with Larry, was green.

As I cleaned it up, Evie touched my hand. "We can't tell anybody."

I nodded in agreement, packed everything up, and drove us across the Canadian border.

Larry had had one last miracle he'd wanted to achieve.

And succeed at it, he did.

No wonder the company wanted him alive.

EPILOGUE

AFTERWORD

This book series began at a time when the whole world felt as though it were ending. I speak, of course, of the lockdown due to the global pandemic.

I'm a professional screenwriter, and the pandemic shut down my industry (along with a legion of others) with no known end in sight. Added to that, most folks had little trust in those in authority and all the existential dread anyone could ever need.

People reacted in unusual ways during this fraught time. Some rebelled and partied (there was a famous street party on Steinway Street in Queens during the height of it, which is still on YouTube), some denied reality, and some hid in fear. Some attacked others who they falsely believed were to blame. It was often ugly.

I sat witness to all of that and had two adolescent sons to entertain and watch over. I told them stories I'd made up, a lot of stories, which I hope lifted their spirits. I like to think so, anyway.

However, I realized that as a writer, I had very little (beyond some film titles, which had only part of my craft on display) to show for my work for the day when I would no longer be around to tell those stories. I wanted to have something to hold in my hand that I could someday give to them. I wanted to pass something along that was solely mine and mine alone, in terms of story.

I had ideas and thoughts that would be more appropriate for them when they were older, and there was no guarantee that I'd be there to share those things when they came of age (again, this was during the pandemic), and that kept me up at night.

Thus, to keep my own mind occupied, I began this series of novellas—to keep my own sanity, to share thoughts and ethics and adventures set in the near future, written specifically for the young men my boys would someday be. I planned to write at least six and even had the covers completed for them ahead of time.

I cracked out three during the lockdown and was halfway through the fourth when a vaccine was found. Once the world began reopening, I finished the fourth and began the fifth.

I finished the fifth and began the sixth, and then the world opened up again. A movie happened, more writing work happened, and that sixth book kept getting put off due to other work and real-world obligations. But I kept chipping away at it.

The world I lived in when I began the series had changed immensely once I reached this book, Volume 6, but echoes reverberated.

The jagged divergence of views, howling about fake news, and the anger and rage on display on January 6 continue to haunt me, and I suspect that they will for quite a long time. The denial of facts (alternative facts) and evidence, the attacks on empathy, left a substantial mark upon the spirit.

While the idea for Jacob the Companion predates the pandemic (I sketched out the idea a long time ago when I thought it might be a good film or show), that traumatic ordeal informed what you've read over six books, though that may be challenging to see upon the surface. But it's there.

The list of titles of creative works wherein Artificial Life and/or Artificial Intelligence rise up to destroy humanity is legion. It struck me that it was less likely that AI would enslave us and more likely that it would be the other way around—people would enslave artificial life. To me, that seems to be the more likely result.

And a horrifying one.

Thus, through Jacob's eyes, I wanted to explore what true humanity is, what makes humans humane, and what makes them cruel and inhuman. I hope you enjoyed his journey thus far, and perhaps we'll see more of him in future stories, too.

Thank you for reading.

Joshua Todd James
May, 2024
Astoria, New York.

ACKNOWLEDGMENTS

Very special thanks to Mom, Dad, brother Stacy, Stephen King for *On Writing* (and many other books, of course), Naomi Wallace, Ato Essandoh, Kevin Jacoby, Keith Link, Todd Alcott, Kristy Elam, Alina Zukurova, Doan Trang, Chad Snopek, Ken Bowser, Marilyn Haft, Matthew Polly, Jim Wright, David Gerrold, Mike Nguyen Le, Scott Myers, Nate Davis, Martin Aguilera, Bill Rodemeyer, Kai Yu Wu, Dwayne Alexander Smith, Joel Eisenberg, Tess Rafferty, Yuri Lowenthal, William C. Martell, Chad Law, Daniel Keys Moran, Sensei Dawn Callan, Sambo Steve, hell, all my dojo pals, the members of the War Room, Julio Gagne, Carlos Sagan, Julio Rivera, Tony Jaa, Mike Selby, Phillip Rhee, Sam Lard & family, and, most importantly, Tomoko Naka and my two ninjas-in-training Kai Naka-James and Ren Naka-James.

ABOUT THE AUTHOR

JOSHUA TODD JAMES is a novelist, screenwriter, and playwright based in New York City. He's written the feature film **Pound Of Flesh**, starring Jean-Claude Van Damme, and the action film **Take Cover**, starring Alice Eve and Scott Adkins, among others. He is a member of WGAE.

Coffee is my co-pilot

Books include THE COMPANION CHRONICLES, which detail the adventures of synthetic person Jacob Kind in the books SOME ANIMALS, MINORITY OF ONE, FREEDOM RUN, MAN IN A BOX, RENEGADE, and DOMO-ARIGATO, MR. ROBOTO. **Joshua Todd James**

ALSO BY JOSHUA TODD JAMES

The Companion Chronicles

SOME ANIMALS - Volume 1

MINORITY OF ONE - Volume 2

FREEDOM RUN - Volume 3

MAN IN A BOX - Volume 4

RENEGADE - Volume 5

DOMO ARIGATO, MR. ROBOTO - Volume 6

And

the collection

THE COMPANION CHRONICLES - Vol 1-3

MINORITY
OF ONE
COMPANION CHRONICLES VOL 2
JOSHUA TODD JAMES

FREEDOM
RUN
COMPANION CHRONICLES VOL 3
JOSHUA TODD JAMES

MAN IN
A BOX
COMPANION CHRONICLES VOL 4
JOSHUA TODD JAMES

RENEGADE
COMPANION CHRONICLES VOL 5
JOSHUA TODD JAMES

DOMO ARIGATO, MISTER ROBOTO
COMPANION CHRONICLES VOL 6
JOSHUA TODD JAMES

www.ingramcontent.com/pod-product-compliance
Lightning Source LLC
LaVergne TN
LVHW050631100826
845148LV00011B/1835

* 9 7 9 8 9 8 5 0 8 7 4 8 2 *